Marie de France
SEVEN OF HER LAYS

Marie de France

SEVEN OF HER LAYS

Done into English by
EDITH RICKERT

London
TIGER OF THE STRIPE
2009

This edition first published
in 2009 by
𝕿iger of the 𝕾tripe
50 Albert Road
Richmond
Surrey TW10 6DP
United Kingdom

ISBN 978-1-904799-45-0

Typeset in the UK by
Tiger of the Stripe
Printed & bound in the US & UK by
Lightning Source

Contents

Preface vii

Introduction ix

Prologue 1

Guigemar 5

The Ash Tree 29

The Two Lovers 45

Yonec 53

The Nightingale 69

The Honeysuckle 75

Eliduc 81

Notes 111

Preface

HE POPULARITY OF Marie de France in her own time was due largely to the fact that she was so entirely in the drift of the literary tendencies of that day. When these had exhausted themselves, she was for centuries almost completely forgotten. During the past hundred years she has been edited, criticised and translated by French and German scholars; but her *Lays*, with two or three exceptions, have remained almost unknown in English.

This fact is the stranger since, in addition to their vivid pictures of perhaps the most attractive period of the Middle Ages, and to a certain charm in the narration, due partly to Celtic origin, partly to Marie herself, the *Lays* have an element of 'humanity,' that is, of appeal to human experience, that seems to make them worth bringing before a wider circle of readers than those who are familiar with twelfth-century French.

In translating, I have endeavoured to keep to the original modes of thought and ways of speech as far as is consistent with a reasonably idiomatic use of modern English; but Marie's language is at once so archaic and so simple, at times almost colloquial, that the way of the translator is hard and craves wary walking. And hence, if I have departed unduly from the modern idiom or from the text, or 'if any one understand it better than' I could, this must be my plea.

I have added a general introduction on Marie's life and work, and separate introductions to the notes on each lay, dealing with the sources, as far as they have been discovered, for the use of students who may not have access to the materials.

Thanks are due to various friends for criticisms upon the translation; and especially to Mr. Alfred Nutt for this, as well as for suggestions in regard to the sources.

With the hope that these tales 'of old unhappy far off things' may find friends among English readers, as they have found admirers in their old French form, this little volume has been prepared.

Mid Yell, Shetland Isles,
August 6, 1901.

Introduction

‘I WILL TELL MY name that I may be remembered: I am called Marie, and I am of France.' This is one of the few definite statements that the most famous writer of mediæval lays makes about herself. She says further: that she has collected and translated her *Lays* in honour of an unnamed 'noble king,' to whom she intends to present them; that she has translated her *Fables*, 'which folk call Esope,' from English, for love of a certain 'Count William,' and that she has turned her *Purgatory of Saint Patrick* into 'Romanz,' 'for the convenience of lay folk.'

Our knowledge of her is somewhat extended by two early allusions. Denis Pyramus, a contemporary, in his *Vie de Saint Edmond*, mentions her immediately after the author of *Partonope*, and in much the same terms. He says:

> And also Dame Marie, who turned into rhyme and made verses of lays which are not in the least true. For these she is much praised, and her rhyme is loved everywhere; for counts, barons, and knights greatly admire it, and hold it dear. And they love her writing so much, and take such pleasure in it, that they have it read and often copied. These lays are wont to please ladies, who listen to them with delight, for they are after their own hearts.

This passage gives a clear impression of Marie's popularity – an impression heightened perhaps by her naïve allusion to her own fame and to the jealousy that it caused (*Guigemar*, p. 7), and by her reference, in the *Epilogue* to the *Fables*, to 'these many clerks' (i.e., scribes), who would like to take to themselves the credit of her work.

The second allusion is in the *Couronnemens Renart*, written after the middle of the thirteenth century. The author states that he is writing in honour of 'Count William, who was formerly Count of Flanders,' and has begun his prologue 'like Marie, who for him treated of Izopet.' This passage, with its apparent identification of Marie's 'Count William' with a Count of Flanders, who from other evidence was Guillaume de Dampierre, (died 1251), misled critics at first as to Marie's date and country; but as the internal evidence in her works speaks decisively for the twelfth century and against Flanders as her home, the only possible conclusion from the passage is that the author was wrong. It may have been a mere accidental blunder on his part; but there are several facts which point towards deliberate falsification. His book was really intended for the younger brother of Guillaume de Dampierre, the Marquis de Namur, whom he wished to instruct in worldly wisdom, and it is followed in the manuscript by Marie's *Fables* (*Izopet*). His statement that he is imitating Marie is fully borne out by the text. In identifying the two counts as one, he seems to try to follow her Anglo-Norman spelling of

the name, having *Williaume* where she has *Willalme*;
but in his conclusion he has the ordinary French form
Guillaume. Again, his phrasing is reminiscent of hers:
her patron is 'flurs – de chevalerie, d'enseignement, de
curteisie,' while the author of *Couronnemens Renart*
speaks of 'la noble chevalerie' of his, calls him 'si sénés,
si larges, si preus, si cortois '; and where Marie's is 'le
plus vaillant de cest reialme,' his is also 'preu vaillant.'
When it is remembered that the poet would doubt-
less win favour from his patron by ascribing to the latter's brother the credit of having inspired so popular
a work as the *Fables*, he can scarcely be acquitted of
either falsifying the facts or of turning his uncertainty
to meet his own ends.

While there is a consensus of opinion among critics today that Marie belongs to the second half of the
twelfth century, there is some difference of opinion as
to the order and more exact placing of her separate
works. Dr. Warnke, who edited the *Fables* in 1898,
and has just brought out a second edition of the Lays
(1901), suggests the following order: (1) the *Lays*, 1160-
70; (2) the *Fables*, 1170–80 5(3) the *Purgatory*, after
1190. It is impossible here to give the various reasons
for this order; but it may be observed that Pyramus
mentions only the *Lays*, while, if we may judge from
the number of manuscripts, the *Fables* came to be
even more popular, and again that Marie's *Prologue*
to the *Lays* seems to imply that this is her first work.

If the identification of Count William with William Longespée (see Page xiii) be correct, the *Fables* were certainly finished after 1170, because at that time he could not have won the position which Marie ascribes to him. And the *Purgatory* was probably written after 1190, since the Latin from which it was translated seems to have been written between 1185 and 1189.* As to Marie's original home, it was either Normandy or that part of the Isle de France which borders upon Normandy. Certain it is, as Professor Suchier suggests, that she shows a closer acquaintance with the little village of Pitres by Pont de l'Arche, near Rouen, than with any other place mentioned in the *Lays*. While as a rule she is content to name her scene, with very little or no description, in *The Two Lovers*, she devotes thirteen lines to a sort of general description of the locality. Further, her descriptions are reasonably accurate: the mountain seems 'marvellous high,' being the last of a range and jutting abruptly out of the plain; the village is not close to the foot of the hill, but is 'near' and 'on one side'; 'in the meadow along the Seine' agrees with local tradition as to the point from which the lovers set out.

Moreover, there are several phrases which seem to show personal acquaintance with the village, such as, 'There is still a town of that name in this place; and indeed the whole country, as we know well, is called the

---

* It is uncertain that *Ille et Galeron*, written about 1167, was based on *Eliduc*. See below, pp. xxv, 146–8..

Vale of Pitres'; and 'There is many a good herb found today.'

On the whole, the claim of Pitres, since it does not conflict with the dialect, is worth attention.

Though when and under what circumstances Marie left France is unknown, it is generally agreed that she did much or all of her literary work in England. This appears from the traces of Anglo-Norman in her dialect, and from her occasional use of English words (such as *nihtegale, gotelef, welke, sepande*), as well as in the fact that she certainly translated her *Fables* from English. Where else could she have learned the language well enough for that purpose? Moreover, by one or two unconscious slips of the pen she strengthens this conclusion. In the *Purgatory* she translates the Latin 'in Angliam redierunt' by 'vindrent aluec en Angleterre,' i.e., she changes 'went back' into 'came hither'; and again in *Milun* she refers to the lands round about Brittany as 'terres de la,' i.e., lands yonder.

The Count William to whom the *Fables* were dedicated probably lived in England, and probably knew little or no English, as the book was translated for him. The man who best answers to Marie's description, 'the most valiant of this realm' and 'the flower of knighthood,' is William Longespée or Longsword (1150–1226), Earl of Salisbury, a natural son of Henry II and Fair Rosamond. Curiously enough, Marie's phrase 'flurs de cheyalrie' is almost the equivalent of one in

the Latin inscription on the earl's tomb in Salisbury
Cathedral, 'flos comitum' (flower of knights).

The king to whom Marie dedicated her *Lays* was
almost certainly Henry II (who reigned 1154–89); and
though we should scarcely accept today her flattering
estimate of his character, he was a generous patron
of literature, as we know from Wace in his *Roman de
Rou*, ll. 5315 ff., 10,455 ff., so that Marie seems justified
in her dedication.

There is nothing in her work to contradict the belief that the title *Dame* bestowed upon her by Denis
Pyramus, indicates that she was a lady of rank. On the
contrary, there is much to confirm it: her education,
the tone of her dedications taken in connection with
the rank of the persons to whom they were addressed,
the refinement of her work, and especially her representation of *l'amour courtois*. This artificial love-code,
based on Ovid as he was understood at that time, for-
mulated in the twelfth century under the direction of
Marie de Champagne, stepdaughter of Henry II, appears in the *Lays* quite as much as in the romances
of Chrétien de Troyes. The atmosphere which Marie
unconsciously reveals in her work is the very court atmosphere of the time.

She was certainly well educated, even bookish, for
her time. She prides herself on her knowledge of Latin
(see *Prologue*); and she certainly knew it well enough
to translate the *Purgatory* with a fair degree of accu-

racy. She knew English at a time when it was a strange tongue, even in England, among the upper classes. It is uncertain whether she knew Welsh or Breton (the use of two Breton words, *bisclavret* and *laustic*, both titles of lays, is very little evidence), and she may easily have derived her materials at second or third hand. She nowhere states that she translates directly from 'Bretun'; she says only that 'li Bretun 'made the lays originally. Still, without being in any sense a scholar, she was a woman of considerable attainment.

A curious change in attitude is observable between the *Lays* and *Fables* on the one hand and the *Purgatory* on the other. In the former she shows no interest in religious matters. In seven of the lays there are no religious allusions, while in the other five they are largely perfunctory. Very few prayers are introduced, and those are as short as possible. By comparing, for instance, the prayers in *Guigemar*, pp. 12, 25, with those of *La Manekine* (ll. 1095–1160 and 4601–4738) by the Sire de Beaumanoir, who was a layman, we see that the latter in describing similar situations of peril introduces prayers of proportionately twice and three times the length of those in *Guigemar*. Again, Marie seems to consider penance a very easy matter (see *The Ash Tree*, page 33); she cannot resist a laugh at the Seigneur of Dol for his donation to the abbey (ib. pp. page 37); she takes the blessing of the archbishop very lightly indeed (ib. page 40); her creed in *Yonec* (page

58) would hardly satisfy the orthodox; and the divorce question in *Eliduc* (page 107) troubles her not at all. It can scarcely be denied that her attitude is thoroughly worldly.

An apparent exception to this statement is found in the conclusion to *Eliduc* (page 108). If it was from remorse that *Eliduc* put his second wife into the convent with his first, and founded for himself another monastery, at least we are not told that this was the reason; it seems rather to be due to the gradual growth of a religious spirit in him as he became older. But in either case, the ending is tacked on so abruptly as to suggest that it was done later by some one who did not approve of the story as it stood.

In *Gilles de Trasignies*, a similar story, the ending is that the second wife at once voluntarily follows the example of the first in entering a convent, and the husband, being deprived of both, does the same. Whether *Gilles* depends upon *Eliduc*, or both go back to a common original, or each has chanced to solve the problem in this way, it is certain at least that both represent a clumsy attempt to fit a non-Christian tale (in that it was originally polygamous, see Notes on *Eliduc*) into the Christian system.

Whether this conclusion was due to Marie's original, or to some monkish copyist, or to Marie herself in later years, cannot perhaps be determined. In favour of the last view may be urged her own change of attitude as seen in the *Purgatory*. Although this is a fairly close translation of the Latin treatise by the monk of Saltrey, there are several indications of a religious attitude on the part of the translator. First, the choice of subject would indicate this; again, though the dedication to some 'bel pere 'is certainly in the original, and refers to the abbot at whose request the book was written, there seems no reason why Marie should have translated it, unless she intended it to refer to some ecclesiastic of her acquaintance, the more so as both her other works have elaborate dedications; and further, among the few lines that she inserts are several that bear out this point of view. There is no word now of her own fame; she is doing this work 'for God.' And in contrast to her allusion in the *Fables* to 'these many clerks,' this poem is done 'that it may be intelligible and suitable to lay folk.'

These reasons, of course, prove nothing more than that, like Denis Pyramus, she turned in her later years from romances to religion; and, one might add, passed through a stage of interest in didactic literature (the *Fables*) between the two. But as Henry II died in 1189, and as she was almost certainly connected with his court, it seems not impossible that she late in life severed her connection with the court, in whatever capacity she was there, and entered a monastery. This is pure conjecture, but it accords with the known facts.

While the *Fables* are interesting chiefly in their relation to Æsop, and the *Purgatory* has its chief value as being a forerunner of the *Divine Comedy*, the *Lays* have a threefold interest: (1) in their relation to ancient folklore, especially Celtic; (2) in their relation to the later romances; (3) in their intrinsic literary value.

The question as to whether the French lays are of Welsh or of Breton origin has become one of the famous battle-grounds in mediæval literature. The early scholars, De la Rue, Roquefort, and others, accepted the word Breton as meaning undoubtedly Armorican; and Villemarqué, when he brought forward his *Barzaz Breiz* as containing the source of one of the lays (*The Nightingale*), maintained this theory. But M. Gaston Paris somewhat later advanced a strong plea in favour of Welsh originals for lost Anglo-Norman poems, themselves the direct sources for the extant lays. Within the last decade a number of German scholars, headed by Professor Zimmer, have returned to the exclusively-Breton theory, supporting their position by philological, geographical, and historical arguments; and these have in turn been attacked by MM. Loth, F. Lot, and others, who, while admitting some of their contentions, hold that both Breton and Welsh materials furnished sources for the lays. (For a brief summary of the main lines of argument, see Bédier, 'Marie de France', *Revue des deux mondes*, tom. 107.)

Dr. Warnke, in his edition of the *Lays* (1901) maintains on the whole the theory of a Breton origin; but the last word has by no means been spoken on the subject.

While it is impossible here even to summarise the various lines of argument adopted, a few facts may be noted which bear upon the question:

1. The history of France and England, of Wales and Brittany, during the twelfth century, shows many points of contact. Henry II continued the conquest of South Wales begun under Henry I. Welshmen fled to their Breton kindred for refuge from the Norman, many indeed being exiled. Further, Henry I spent most of the latter part of his life in France, and Henry II carried out a continuous and in the end fairly successful warfare of subjugation in Brittany. Henry's son Geoffrey married Constance, the heiress of Brittany, and became reigning duke, to whom all the native seigneurs were forced to do homage. The English were at Nantes, at Dol, at St. Michel. The English court was held frequently for months in the various Breton towns. It seems inevitable that under such conditions there should have been a very extensive interchange of ideas and stories among these races. Further, a bit of evidence to show the Welsh influence may be given from Giraldus Cambrensis, *Itinerarium Cambriæ*, lib. I., cap. 1. 150

Here we find the closest parallel to Marie's story of the hind with stag's horns, who, when shot, afflicted her slayer with blindness in the right eye and with paralysis. Giraldus adds that he had the story from one who knew the man, and also that the head and horns of the strange beast were taken to Henry II. The story may be a mere fabrication, based on earlier fairy tales of the sort, which are found especially in Irish literature; but the fact remains that it is associated with Wales and with Henry II.

2. The tendency of popular literature is to accumulate and assimilate to itself elements from all other popular literatures with which it comes historically into contact. Granted the continued association of the English Normans with both Bretons and Welsh, it seems impossible to limit their sources to either the one or the other people.

3. The evidence of the lays themselves is in favour of a two-fold origin. As to scene, they vary: *Guigemar* in its names of persons and places seems purely Breton, while *The Honeysuckle* seems purely Welsh. The scene of *Equitan*, *The Unfortunate*, *The Ash Tree*, *The Nightingale*, and *The Werewolf* is Brittany; but the localisation does not extend beyond the bare mention of a name here and there. The weight of evidence for *Yonec* and *Lanvall* seems to point towards Great Britain (though the hero of the variant *Grælent* in the case of the latter is distinctly Breton). In *Milun* and *Eliduc* the

scene shifts from Great Britain to Brittany and *vice versa*, the former hero being a native of South Wales, the latter of Brittany; but it should be noted that here, in both cases, the more definite descriptions deal with Great Britain. The *Two Lovers* is Norman. (See Notes on the separate lays.)

4. The sources of the lays, so far as it is possible to determine them by a comparison of parallel versions, are certainly, in large measure, Celtic, but by no means exclusively Breton. It may be due to accidents of preservation that Irish literature furnishes the largest number of parallels, Welsh next, while Breton and Scots-Gælic can give nothing more than isolated suggestions; still the fact rather makes against the exclusively Breton theory. (See Notes as above.)

The form of the original sources has been discussed largely. It is agreed that they were as a rule popular folk-stories, adapted for the court circles of the twelfth century; but the number of siftings, of revisions, of additions, compressions, mutilations, alterations and combinations that they passed through before Marie gave them their present shape, it is impossible at present to determine. At first one is inclined to make the number large; but after comparing with Marie, on the one hand the primitive Irish tales of the *Silva Gadelica*, and on the other the fully developed romances of *Ille et Galeron* and *Galerent de Bretagne*, both dating from the twelfth century, one is inclined to emphasize the difference between the lays and romances rather than that between the lays and early folk-tales. Marie's poems contain, to a far larger degree than do the romances, traces of their Celtic originals in their delicate grace and simplicity and child-like *naïveté*, though it is also true that the primitive barbaric elements have been largely eliminated.

Still they are undoubtedly several removes from the Celtic materials. In holding this, it is not necessary to question Marie's truthfulness, for though she often says that 'li Bretun' made them, and that she has heard them (and sometimes read them) she never once makes the claim that she herself got them from the Britons.

Did Marie's material reach her in the form of verse or prose? The theory set forth by M. Bédier (*Revue des deux mondes*, tom. 107, p. 849 ff.) and by Dr. Warnke (second edition of the *Lays*), seems to accord best with the known facts. This is briefly: that the narrative lays in Marie have developed out of an early form, in which the story was told in prose, and the emotions of the characters, usually in the form of a speech, were expressed in a short lyric, the prose being spoken, the poetry sung; that it was the music that first attracted the French minstrels, and roused curiosity as to the meaning; and since it would have been extremely difficult for them to render the verse adequately into French verse, it came about that the prose parts were done into verse, while the lay itself was either entirely omitted or embodied in a greatly altered or compressed state.

There is abundant evidence as to the lyric character of the original lays. I shall quote only *Galerent de Bretagne*, ll. 7010–15:

> Nor did he fail to know both words and music, the note of *Galeren le Breton*. And all the ladies and knights hearkened to it, though none understood the delight of the words save they two (i.e., who knew Breton); but the song was sweet and made them all listen.

Further, Gottfried von Strassburg mentions a Welsh and an Irish harper as playing Breton lays. Giraldus Cambrensis, *Descrip. Camb.*, lib. I, cap. xii, testifies to Welsh 'cantilenis rhythmicis' (rhythmic songs) and to the fame of Welsh music; and a singing contest of minstrels, a sort of early *eisteddfod*, at the court of Prince Rhys in 1177, is mentioned in the Welsh *Chronicle* (quoted by Hoare, ed. Gir. Camb., II, p. 53).

Again, this prose and verse form blended is common in the early Irish stories, the only Celtic tales which in their existing form antedate the twelfth century. In the *Silva Gadelica*, the singing of a *laoid*, a short lyric expression of the speaker's emotions, occurs very often.

Lastly, this explanation makes clear several puzzling statements in the little introductions and conclusions of Marie. It explains her use of the word *rhyme*, her apparent distinction between *conte* or narrative and

lay, her use of the expression 'I have heard *told*' (*conté*).
It explains: 'The stories (*contes*) that I know to be true,
of which the Britons have made lays, I will tell you'
(*conterai*), when taken in connection with 'Of this *conte* that you have heard, was made the *Lay of Guigemar*
which is told to the harp and to the rote – sweet is
the music thereof'; also, 'I will tell you the *Lay of the
Ash*, according to the *cunte* that I know'; and 'He who
would treat of various stories' (*cuntes*), and 'Of their
love and weal, the ancients made a lay, and I who have
put it into writing, take great pleasure in retelling it'
(*recunter*). But the two most interesting passages are
in *The Unfortunate* and in *The Honeysuckle*. In the former we have the description of the making of a lay,
which could have been little more than a lament. The
lady says: 'In that I have loved you all so much, I will
that my grief be remembered. Of you four I will make
a lay and call it *Quatre Doels*' (*four woes*, or, perhaps,
elegies?). The knight bids her make it over again and
call it *The Unfortunate*, because he alone is unhappy;
his three companions have died gloriously, while he
was only wounded and lives to look upon her whom
he loves so dearly, and yet cannot win her love. Clearly
Marie does not attempt to give even the substance of
the lay, she gives only 'the adventure' upon which it
was founded; she tells how it came to be made, and
how it was changed (for the lady accepts the knight's
emendation). Again, in *The Honeysuckle*, Marie claims

distinctly that she is only telling *how, by whom* and *of what* the lay was made.

It seems probable then that the French lays were rhymed out of prose stories which contained lyrics called lays; and that the French versions were so named partly because it was the lyric lays that especially attracted the French audience, and partly because they also were in verse form. Perhaps *Aucassin and Nicolete* represents, in some degree, the song-story form of the originals.

That the French lays themselves were sung with a definite melody, it is impossible to believe; that they were given in a sort of chant, with some musical accompaniment, is probable.

The influence of Marie's lays upon the development of mediæval literature was at first considerable. They were in the drift of the tendencies of that time, as is shown perhaps by the fact that her stories of *Lanvall* and *Milun* are repeated in the anonymous lays, *Grælent* and *Doon*. The Honeysuckle, indeed, appears to be merely an offshoot of the Tristan legend; but *The Ash Tree* is the source for the romance of *Galerent de Bretagne* while *Eliduc* is akin to the source for the romance of *Ille and Galeron*. Aside from these facts, *Guigemar* and *Eliduc* by their length and complexity suggest the evolution of the lay into the romance. As we have no manuscript of the *Lays* later than the beginning of the fourteenth century, we may conclude that their popularity was exhausted by that time, or rather that they were superseded by the romances which they had helped to develop.

All of Marie's lays except *Eliduc* were translated into Norse about the middle of the thirteenth century. Until recent times only two have been done into English, *The Ash Tree* about 1300, and *Lanvall* no less than three times during the fourteenth and fifteenth centuries.

With the awakening interest in things mediæval towards the close of the eighteenth century began the critical study of the life and work of Marie de France. The writings of Le Grand d'Aussy, Roquefort, Robert and De la Rue were followed by those of Mall and Warnke.

While many eminent critics today busy themselves with the problems of Marie's life and work, very few attempts at translation or imitation have been made. In 1816, Miss Matilda Betham published a poem entitled *Lay of Marie*, in which a purely fictitious account of the mediæval poet is given. In an appendix she gives Way's metrical translation of *Guigemar* and *Lanvall* (from his *Fabliaux*), and Scott's prose version of *The Honeysuckle* (appendix to *Sir Tristrem*). In 1872, Mr. O'Shaughnessy published free metrical versions, with much additional material, of several of the lays, but they afford little conception of the originals. Miss

Weston has included *Lanvall* and *The Werewolf* in her collection of *Four French Lais*, 1900.[*]

In determining the intrinsic merit of the lays, it is necessary first to endeavour to put aside the qualities due to the originals, and then to judge of their worth from the standpoint of revelation of personality and of the artistic skill shown in the treatment.

It is by a comparison of the early Celtic tales with the fully-developed romances of Marie's own time that we are enabled to put aside the qualities of style to which she may not lay credit. Further, judging by her literal rendering of the Purgatory, we must expect to find her peculiarities in the little unconscious touches and expressions of sympathy rather than in a definite theory of modification of her sources. While we may not credit her with the dainty bits of nature and little scenes from life scattered throughout the lays, we may praise her judgment for keeping them (though, to be sure, we do not know how many others she has omitted); and further, we can praise the discretion and restraint which kept her from over-embroidering with incongruous details the delicate fancies of her originals. Whether it is from a sense of duty to her originals, or from a natural simplicity of mind, as opposed to the subtlety of Chrétien de Troyes or Benoît de Sainte-More, she has a child-

[*]   Arthurian Romances unrepresented in Malory, No. 3. A translation of *Eliduc* by Mrs. Kemp-Welch has appeared in the *Monthly Review*, July, 1901.

like delight in the external and tangible, in the story for itself, that is rather refreshing in an age over-fond of analysing situations and states of mind. The sentimentality to which M. Bédier attributes her popularity among women seems to me a quality of the subject-matter, the treatment being brusque, and at times almost flippant.

Whatever her rank and position may have been, she is essentially aristocratic in her tastes; she is imbued with the ideals of chivalry, with its rigid standards of courtesy and its un-modern morality; she does not escape, superficially, the impress of the Church. Yet when we examine these qualities, we see that they need further modification. Here and there we find gleams of sympathy with 'poor peasant folk'; again her conception of *l'amour courtois*, complete as it is, is not altogether orthodox. Usually she favours the lovers as against the husband – one of the fundamental principles of *l'amour courtois* being that the husband could not continue to be the lover – but in *Equitan* and *The Werewolf* she distinctly condemns the wife's treachery, seeming also to disapprove of her intrigue, while in *Eliduc*, the hero has most modern ideas on the duty of conjugal faithfulness. And as to religion, it was quite unimportant to her until she wrote the *Purgatory*.

She is French in her light-heartedness, which now and then is touched with a dash of wit or a delicate bit of humour, as in her account of Gurun's generosity in

The Ash Tree, and of the old porter, or her description of the lovers in *The Nightingale*.

On the whole, the impression one gets is of a clever, lively woman, delicate-minded yet not too orthodox, with no great power of originality, who being quite aware of her knack of saying things prettily, turns to literature partly as a pastime and partly out of ambition.

That she had an ideal appears from the introduction to *Guigemar*; that she worked hard, from this as well as from the *Prologue*. Yet, while the first impression which one derives from the lays is one of charm, due perhaps to the clear-cut pictures and fitness of the phrasing to the ideas, structurally they are not 'well told.'

They show the lack of unifying power, so common a defect in mediæval narratives; the various elements in the plot are often badly combined, the centre of interest is shifted unskilfully at times, and on the whole we feel that it is brevity of material perhaps rather than artistic skill in handling it, that saves Marie from the exaggerated faults of some of her contemporaries.

The characters are largely conventional? there is a fixed type of physical and spiritual qualities for hero, heroine, and villain. Yet at intervals we find flashes of insight into human nature, some of them so unimportant to the tale that they would seem to be Marie's own; such as, the laugh of the angry husband in

The Nightingale, the mutual shyness of the lovers and Guilliadun's reception of the chamberlain in *Eliduc,* the finding of the waif in *The Ash Tree,* and the guilty mother's feeling when she recognises her daughter, in the same poem.

Smoothness, lightness, and ease in managing her verse – the common octosyllabic rhyming couplet of the time, perhaps best represented in English by Chaucer's later *Dethe of Blaunche the Duchesse* – Marie shared with most of her contemporaries. Compared with the exquisite Tightness of *Aucassin and Nicolete,* her Lays seem artificial, while set over against the gorgeous and elaborate fancies of Chrétien de Troyes, they seem almost childishly simple. But she had some poetic instinct and some experience of life in the most brilliant period of the Middle Ages; moreover, she had a pretty gift of miniature painting, a clever touch in phrasing, the wisdom to choose ancient folk-tales, beautiful in themselves, and the patience to remould them conscientiously and to 'wake nights' in the work. The results were perhaps not unworthy of the great king to whom they were presented.

PROLOGUE

E TO WHOM God has granted wisdom and eloquence in speech ought not to hide these gifts in silence, but gladly to make use of them; for when a goodly thing is much talked of, then first is it in blossom, and when it is praised of many, then only has it unfolded its flowers.

Priscian tells us that it was the custom of the ancients to speak obscurely in their books, that men of later days, who should learn them, might employ the whole resources of their wit in expounding the text, for the philosophers knew by their own experience that the more folk gave their time to this, the more subtle of wit they would become, and hence the better able to guard against that which should be avoided. And, indeed, if any one would keep himself from sin, he should study and learn and undertake a wearisome task; in this way he may spare himself great sorrow.

This is how I came to think of translating some good history from Latin into Romance; but so many others have undertaken to do this that it would have been no credit to me. Then I bethought me of the lays that I had heard. I knew well, beyond a doubt, that they who first made them and sent them into the world did this in remembrance of the adventures they had heard; and, as I have heard many of them told and would not have them forgotten, I have rhymed them into verses – and many a night have I waked over it!

In honour of you, noble King, moſt excellent and gracious, to whom all joy does homage, and in whose heart all good has root, I have set about gathering lays, and retelling them in rhyme. I said in my heart, sire, that I would offer them to you; and if it pleases you to accept them, you will give me such great joy that I shall be glad ever after. Think me not overbold in offering you this gift!

Now hearken, and I will begin:

GUIGEMAR

NE WHO IS treating of good matter is troubled if it be not well done; but hearken, lords, to Marie, who uses her time as well as she may. Such an one, who is talked of for her good work, ought to be praised of folk; but, indeed, wherever there is a man or woman of great fame, those who are envious of her good work often slander her, and with the intent to lessen her fame play the part of a wretched, cowardly dog, a cur that bites folk stealthily. But I will not leave off for this, even though backbiters and false flatterers work mischief against me – for to speak ill is their nature.

I will tell you as shortly as I can the stories that I know to be true, whereof the Britons have made lays. And in the beginning I will set before you as briefly as possible, according to the letter of the writing, an adventure which befel in Britain-the-Less, in days of old.

In that time Hoilas held the land, often in peace and often in war. Among his barons was a lord of Léon, called Oridials, whom he loved especially. This worthy and valiant knight had by his wife two children, a son and a fair daughter. The damsel was named Noguent, and the lad, who was the prettiest boy in all that realm, Guigemar. His mother loved him to a marvel, and his father set great store by him.

Yet as soon as he could bear to part with the lad, he sent him to serve the king at court. Guigemar, being gentle and of good wit, was soon beloved by all; and when he came to be of proper age and understanding, the king dubbed him with due honours and gave him arms at his will.

Thereupon Guigemar, after scattering largesse freely, departed from the court and went to Flanders, where there was always strife and war, to win him glory. Neither in Lorraine nor in Burgundy, in Anjou nor in Gascony, at that time could be found his peer among knights. Yet he perverted nature in so far that he cared nothing for love. There was no dame or damsel under heaven, however noble or however fair, who would not at his entreaty have yielded him her love; nay, more, many often sought him, but he had no liking thereto. It did not appear that he would have aught to do with love; hence, friends and strangers alike held him to be in perilous case.

In the flower of his fame, the knight returned to his own land, to visit his father and his liege-lord, his good mother and his sister, all of whom had greatly longed for him; and he tarried with them, I trow, a whole month.

One evening the wish seized him to go a-hunting, so he sent for his knights, his hunters, and his beaters, and in the morning went into the forest – for this sport pleased him mightily!

They got track of a great stag; the dogs were uncoupled; the hunters ran forward; the young knight followed more slowly, for a servant bore his bow and quiver and hanger, and he wished to shoot, if a chance offered, before he went further.

Presently he beheld in a thicket of dense underbrush a hind with her fawn; she was all white and had the horns of a ſtag upon her head. When at the brachet's baying she came forth, he ſtretched his bow and drew upon her, piercing her in the fore part of the hoof so that she ſtraightway fell. But the arrow rebounded and pierced his thigh even to the saddle, in such wise that it brought him quickly to the ground. He fell to the earth on the soft grass beside the wounded hind. She was hurt sorely, and moaning with pain, ſpoke in this manner: 'Oï! Alas! I am slain! and thou, vassal, who haſt wounded me, be thy fate such that never shalt thou find cure. Be it that neither herb nor root, nor the potion of any leech, shall help thee of the wound in thy thigh until thou art healed by a woman, who for love of thee shall suffer such pain and such sorrow as never woman has had before; and thou shalt bear as much for her – whereat shall marvel all who love, and have loved, and shall love ever after. Get thee hence, and leave me in peace!'

Guigemar, as he lay there sorely wounded, was horror-ſtruck at these words, and bethought him into what land he should go for the healing of his wound, since he was loth to die. He knew well enough, and told himself, that never had he seen woman whom he could love, who therefore should heal him of his pain. But calling his varlet he said:

'Friend, put spurs to thy horse and bid my comrades return, for I would speak with them.'

The man spurred away; and Guigemar, though crying out for anguish, bound the wound tightly with his tunic, then mounted and rode on. In his fear that he might meet some of his men to stop him, or at least delay him, it seemed long ere he was thence.

Midway through the forest a grassy road led him out of the woodland; and in the plain below he beheld the banks and cliffs of a river, an arm of the sea, which formed there a harbour. In this was a single ship of which he could see the mast. Right seaworthy was that boat, so well pitched within and without that no seam could be found; all its pegs and fittings were of ebony, as precious as any gold under heaven, and its unfurled sail was of most lovely silk.

The knight bethought him that he had never heard tell of a ship landing in these parts; but none the less he advanced and climbed down to the barque. Though with grievous pain to his wound, he went on board, thinking to find there those who had charge of the ship; but he saw no one.

Amid the vessel he came upon a bed, whereof the feet and sides were Solomon's work, of cypress and white ivory inlaid with gold. The quilt was of silk and gold tissue; the other fittings I scarcely know how to praise; but this much will I tell you of the pillow: whoso placed his head upon it should never have grey hair. The coverlet was of sable and lined with Alexandrian purple. In the prow of the boat were set two candlesticks of fine gold (the worse worth a treasure-hoard), in which were two lighted tapers.

Marvelling greatly at all this, he lay down upon the bed to rest a while, for his wound pained him. But when he arose presently to depart, he might not return, for the vessel was speeding away with him on the high seas, before a soft, favouring wind, that left no hope of retreat. 'Tis no marvel that he was anxious and ill at ease, for his wound hurt him grievously and he knew not what to do. Yet he must go through with the adventure; so, praying God to keep watch over him, and in His might to bring him to some haven and save him from death, he lay down on the bed again and fell asleep.

To-day he has borne the worst of his destiny; before evensong he shall arrive where he is to be healed, below the walls of an ancient city, the capital of that kingdom.

Now the lord who ruled this city was a very old man, and had to wife a lady of high lineage, gentle, courteous, fair and discreet. But he was jealous out of all measure, for so are all old men by nature, each dreading mightily lest he be deceived – 'tis the way of age!

No laughing matter was the watch that he kept over her! At the foot of the donjon was a garden shut in on all sides. The walls were of green marble, wondrous high and thick, with but one entrance, and that guarded night and day. On the fourth side was the sea, so that none who must needs to the castle might enter there, or depart, save it were by boat.

Here within, this lord, for the safekeeping of his wife, had built the fairest chamber under heaven, and at its entrance a chapel. The room was all adorned with paintings; and among other things was a representation of Venus, the Goddess of Love, showing the ways and nature of love, how folk should hold fast to it, and serve the goddess well and faithfully. She was casting into a blazing fire Ovid's book, wherein he teaches men to eschew love; and, furthermore, was cursing all who should ever read that book or obey its precepts.

In this chamber was the lady imprisoned. Her husband placed with her, as attendant, his niece, his sister's child, a maiden of noble birth and breeding. Between these two ladies was great love, and whenever the lord was away, they were always together until he returned. Besides this damsel no other person entered within the wall or issued thence, save an old priest, grey and ripe of years, who had the key of the postern and went in to read God's service before the lady, and to wait upon her at table.

This self-same day, in the early afternoon, the lady, attended by her maiden, went into the garden. She had been sleeping after her mid-day meal, and now went out to amuse herself. Looking down towards the sea, they beheld a ship breasting the flood and sailing into the harbour, yet saw no means whereby it was conveyed thither.

The lady, blushing rosily, turned to flee – 'tis no marvel that she was afraid – but the damsel, who was quick-witted and bolder of heart, comforted her and reassured her so that they soon went down together. The maiden, putting aside her mantle, entered the wondrous skiff, but found therein no living creature save the sleeping knight. She paused there and looked at him, and, seeing him all pale, believed that he was dead. So she went back and quickly called her lady, telling her what she had seen, with piteous lament for the dead.

The lady answered: 'Let us go to him. If he is dead our priest will help us to bury him; and if I find him alive he will surely speak to us.'

With no delay they passed down together into the boat, the lady going first. When she had entered the skiff, she paused before the bed and gazed upon the knight, often lamenting the fairness of his form, for it seemed to her that his youth was come to naught; and she was sorrowful for him. But when she put her hand on his breast she felt it warm, and all sound the heart

[13]

that beat against his side. And thereupon the sleeping knight waked and saw her, and greeted her with much joy, perceiving that he was come to land. The lady, who had been weeping sadly for him, answered him with all kindness, and then asked him how he had come, and from what land, and whether he was exiled through war.

'By no means, lady,' said he. 'But if it please you to hear my adventure, I will tell it and hide nothing. I am of Britain-the-Less, and to-day I went a-hunting in the woods, where I shot a white hind. But the arrow flew back and wounded me in the thigh – and never may I hope to be healed! The hind made moan and with bitter curses spoke, vowing that never should I have remedy save through a maiden whom I know not where to find! When I heard my fate I came at once out of the wood, and seeing this vessel entered therein (fool that I was!) and the boat fled away with me; I know not where I am arrived, nor what is the name of this city. Fair lady, for God's sake, I pray you of your grace, give me counsel, for I know not whither to go, nor can I steer my skiff!'

She made answer: 'Fair sir and dear, gladly will I give you counsel. This city is my husband's, and all the land round about. He is a mighty man of high degree, but of age right ancient, and, by my faith, bitterly jealous! He has shut me within this close with its one entrance, where an old priest guards the door. May God grant that he burn in hell-fire! Here am I imprisoned night and day; and never at any time should I dare to go forth unless he give me leave, or my lord summon me. Here have I my chamber and my chapel, and this maiden to serve me; and if it please you to tarry until you are better able to journey, gladly will we entertain you and serve you with good will!'

Upon these words the knight thanked the lady sweetly, and said that he would remain with her. Then he raised himself on the bed, and they helped him as they could.

Thus they led him into the lady's chamber, and placed him on the damsel's bed, behind a rich tapestry which they devised as a curtain in the room. In basins of gold they brought water, and bathed the wound in his thigh, first staunching the blood with a fair cloth of white linen; then they bandaged it tightly, dealing with him in all tenderness.

When their supper came, at eventide, the maiden kept enough for the knight also, and he ate and drank heartily.

But Love had pierced him to the quick, and set his heart in a tumult; for the lady had so bewitched him that he quite forgot his native land, and though he felt no pain from his hurt, he sighed in sore anguish, and begged the maiden, who was to serve him, that she leave him alone to sleep. So she went away to her lady, who was also in some degree touched by the fire which so enkindled and inflamed the knight's heart.

He remained alone, pensive and heavy-hearted, though not yet knowing why; still, he perceived well that if he were not healed by this lady, his death was assured.

'Alas!' said he, 'what shall I do? I will go to her and ask her to have mercy and pity on this despairing wretch. If she refuse my prayer, and be proud and cruel, then must I either die or languish all my life with this wound!'

Thereupon he sighed; but in a little while made a new resolve, even to bear it, for so does he who can no better.

All that night he wakened, in sighing and in sore trouble, remembering in his heart her words and her manner, her shining eyes and her sweet mouth, that had brought this sorrow into his heart! Between his teeth he cried out for mercy – almost called her his love!

If he had known how she too was overcome by love he would have been right glad, I trow! Even a little relief would have lessened somewhat the woe that made him all pale.

But if he was suffering for love of her, she indeed had no reason to boast. She arose in the morning ere dawn, complaining that love so overwhelmed her that she could not sleep.

Her maiden knew well by her manner that she loved this knight now tarrying in her chamber until he should be healed; but she knew not whether he loved the lady or no. So when the dame was gone to the chapel, her maiden went and sat down by the knight's bed, whereupon he called her, saying:

'Friend, whither is my lady gone? Why is she arisen so early?' No more than this he said, yet he sighed.

Said the damsel: 'Sir, you are in love! Now see to it that you hide it not overmuch. It may be that your love is well bestowed. The man whom my lady would love ought verily to hold her in high honour; yet, if you both should be constant, your love would be most fitting, for you are fair and she is fair!'

He answered the maid: 'I am so overcome by love that I am surely undone, unless I have succour or aid. Counsel me, my sweet friend! What shall I do with this love?'

She comforted him with great sweetness, and assured him that she would aid him as most she might; for she was indeed courteous and debonair.

When the lady had heard mass she came back, yet could not forget. She was eager to know how he did, whom she could not cease to love, and whether he waked or slept. And at once the damsel called her forth to come to the knight that she might at leisure show him all her heart, turn it to weal or woe.

They greeted each other, shyly both. He scarcely dared entreat her, for he was a stranger, and feared that if he showed her his trouble she might hate him and drive him away. Yet he who shows not his sickness may not be cured! Love is a wound within the heart; and if it may not win its way out, 'tis an ill that lasts long, because it comes of Nature. Many hold it a light thing, like these churls that call themselves knights, who seek their own pleasure through the world, then boast of their evil deeds. This is not love, but rather folly, sin, and lechery. Whoever finds a true lover ought faithfully to serve and love and obey him. Now Guigemar loves so exceedingly, that, whether he is destined to have speedy help or to live against his will, love gives him courage to lay bare his heart.

'Lady,' he said, 'I am dying for love of you! My heart is so tortured that unless you will heal me I must verily die! I would have you for my lady; sweet, do not say me nay!'

When she had heard this, she answered modestly, though all smiling: 'Friend, 'twould be rather too soon to grant your prayer; I am not wont so to do!'

'Lady,' he pleaded, 'for God's sake, be not angry at what I shall tell you! 'Tis well enough for a light woman to make herself long entreated; it will increase her value to be thought unused to love. But the pure-hearted woman, who is virtuous and of good discretion, if she find a man to her liking ought not to treat him too haughtily before she consent to love him. Before any one should know or hear of it, they might have much joy together. Fair lady, let us end this debate!'

She knew that his words were true, and granted him her love, whereupon he kissed her and henceforth was well at ease, as they dallied and spoke together, with kisses and embraces. Surely it is fitting that they should have a just share of what other folk are wont to have!

'Tis my belief that Guigemar was with her a year and a half, living in great joy. But Fortune is not idle; nay, in a little while turns her wheel, putting one up and another down. So it was with them, for presently they were discovered.

One morning in the springtide, as the lady lay beside her knight, she kissed his lips and his face, saying: 'Fair sweet love, my heart tells me that I shall lose you; we shall be spied upon and discovered. If you die, I would fain die; but if you can escape you may find another love, and I shall abide desolate!'

'Lady,' said he, 'no more of this. Never should I have joy or peace with any woman but yourself! Have no fear!'

'Friend, that I may be sure of this, let me take your tunic and plait in it a fold below the lappet in such wise that if any woman can undo it, or know how to take out the fold, her you may love with my consent.'

[19]

He gave it to her, with assurances of his faith; and she made the plait in such manner that no woman could undo it, unless she used force or knife.

And when she returned the tunic, he took it upon the covenant that he might also be assured of her by means of a girdle. Whoso could open the buckle thereof, without breaking it or injuring it, him might she well love. Thereupon he kissed her, and with that was content.

This very day they were observed and discovered by a chamberlain of evil cunning, whom his lord had sent thither to speak with the lady. He might not enter into the chamber, but he saw them through a window, and returned to tell his lord.

When the baron heard this he was more sorrowful than ever before in his life. Calling three of his trusty men, he went suddenly to the chamber, and bade them break down the door; and when he found the knight within, in his great fury told them to slay him. Guigemar rose to his feet, no whit a-dread. He seized in both hands a great beam of pine, on which clothes usually hung – so awaited them, thinking to make them sorry one and all; nay, to cripple them, every man, ere they could approach him!

The baron looked at him hard, then asked him who he was, of what race, and how he had come there within. Guigemar told how he had arrived and how the lady had kept him – told all his fate, of the wounded

hind, of the skiff, and of his own hurt, confessing that
now is he utterly in the baron's power.

The lord answered that he did not believe him; yet
if it were indeed as he had said, and the boat could be
found, let him put it to sea again; and if he were saved
'twere pity, but if he drowned, well.

The knight assured him once more. They went
down together, found the vessel, launched it, and it
departed with Guigemar to his own land.

The skiff stayed not at all, but floated away, while
the knight sighed and wept for his lady, and prayed
God Omnipotent to grant him speedy death, and let
him never come to port unless he might have his lady,
whom he loved more than his life. In this sorrow he
continued until the vessel had come to the harbour
where first he had found it, hard by his own domain.

Thereupon he disembarked at once, and beheld a
squire, whom he had nurtured, riding after a knight
and leading a horse. Guigemar knew him and called
him by name; and the lad, looking up and seeing his
liege lord, dismounted and offered him the horse.
They then went away together.

Joyous were all Guigemar's friends at his return, and
held him in high honour throughout the land; but he
was ever sorrowful and distraught, and when they
urged him to marry refused utterly, saying that never
would he take wife either for treasure or for love, unless she could unplait the fold in his tunic without

tearing it. These tidings went through all Brittany; and there was neither dame nor damsel who did not go thither to essay it, yet none could undo it.

But now I must tell you of the lady whom Guigemar loved so dearly. Her husband, by the counsel of one of his barons, imprisoned her in a tower of grey marble, where ill was the day and the night worse. No man in the world could tell the great grief and the sorrow, the anguish and the woe, that she suffered in her tower for two years and more, I ween, with no joy or pleasure whatsoever. Again and again she made moan for her lover: 'O Guigemar, my lord, woe that ever I saw you! 'Tis better to die at once than to bear long such sorrow as mine! If only I might escape, love, I would drown myself even where you were cast into the sea!'

Thereupon she arose and in her despair went to the door. Lo! she found there nor key nor lock; by good fortune passed out without hindrance, so came to the harbour, and even as she was about to drown herself, found the skiff fastened to a rock. She entered therein, thinking only how her lover had been drowned here; and as she remembered, she could no longer stand, but even as she reached the brink, stumbled and fell forward into the boat. Heavy indeed was her sorrow and grief!

The skiff floated away, and bore her quickly thence to a port in Brittany, below a strong and splendid castle.

Now the lord of this castle, who was called Meriadus, was making war on one of his neighbours, and arose in the morning betimes to send out his men to attack his foe. He was standing by the window and saw the skiff arrive; and thereupon, calling his chamberlain, he descended the stairs and came at once to the vessel. They climbed aboard by means of a ladder, and found within the lady, who was lovely as a fay. He took her up in her mantle and bore her with him to his castle, greatly rejoicing in his treasure-trove, for she was fair beyond the telling. Whoever had put her in the skiff, Meriadus knew well that she was of gentle birth, and straightway loved her with such love that never had any woman greater.

He commended her to his sister, who was a right fair maid. She took the lady into her bower, where she was well served and honoured, richly arrayed and adorned; but yet she was ever pensive and mournful.

The lord himself went often to speak with her, for he loved her with fair intent; yet much as he sought her, she never took heed save to show him the girdle, saying that she would love only him who could undo it without breaking. Hearing this, he answered with ill humour:

MARIE DE FRANCE

'Likewise there is in this land a knight of great renown, who saves himself from taking wife, by means of a plait in the right lappet of his tunic, which may not be undone unless knife or force be put to it. You have made that plait, I trow!'

At these words she sighed and almost swooned, whereupon he caught her in his arms, severed the lace of her robe, and strove to unclasp the girdle, but might not succeed. Afterwards was there no knight in that land, whom he did not make to essay it.

Thus matters stood for a long time until it befel that Meriadus entered into a tournament with his enemy. And so he summoned many knights, and first among them Guigemar, to whom he offered guerdon if he would stand by him in this stour, and would bring friends and comrades to succour him. Hence Guigemar went thither in rich array, taking more than an hundred knights.

Meriadus entertained him with great honour in his castle. He sent word by two knights to his sister that she should attire herself duly and come forth to meet the guest, and bring also the lady whom he loved so well; and she did as he commanded.

In their splendid attire they came hand in hand into the hall. And when this pale and pensive lady heard *Guigemar's* name she could scarce stand; indeed, if the other had not held her she would have fallen to the floor.

The knight rose to meet them, but when he saw the lady, ſtudied her face and her bearing, and drew back a little, saying to himself:

'Is this my sweet friend, my hope, my heart, my life, my dear lady who loves me? Whence is she come? Who brought her hither? Now verily I am thinking nonsense, for I know well that it cannot be she – women are much alike! My thoughts are ſtirred in vain, because this woman only resembles her for whom my heart longs and sighs. Yet will I ſpeak to her gladly!'

Then he advanced and kissed her, and sat down by her side, though he ſpoke no word beyond asking leave to sit there.

Meriadus watched them, sorely troubled at their looks, yet said to Guigemar, with a laugh:

'Sir, so please you, this damsel will essay to unplait your tunic, if perchance she may succeed.'

He answered, 'I grant this,' and calling the chamberlain, who had charge of the tunic, bade him bring it. But when it was given to the maiden in no wise might she undo it.

The lady knew the fold well, and her heart beat wildly for her eagerness to make the essay, if she might, or dared. Meriadus perceiving this, was sorrowful as never before, yet said:

'Dame, do you now try if you can unplait it.'

When she heard this command, she took hold of the lappet of the tunic, and undid it easily.

The knight marvelled, for, though he knew her well, he could not bring himself to believe fully, and spoke to her in this wise:

'Love, sweet thing, is it you? Tell me truly! Let me see the girdle wherewith I girt you.'

Putting his arms about her, he felt the girdle, and said further:

'Sweet, what a strange chance that I have found you thus! Who brought you hither?'

She told him all the sorrow and the anguish and the woe of the prison where she had been, how at length she had escaped and would have drowned herself, but chanced upon the skiff, entered it, and was borne away to this castle. Here the knight had maintained her in great honour, though he was always seeking her love – but now is all her joy returned! 'Friend, take away your lady!'

Guigemar rose to his feet and said: 'Hearken to me, sir. I have found here my dear lady whom I thought to have lost. I ask and implore you, Meriadus, of your mercy to give her up to me, and I will become your liegeman and serve you two years or three with an hundred knights or more.'

Then Meriadus answered: 'Guigemar, my good friend, I am no longer so oppressed or burdened by any war that you should ask this of me. I found the lady and I will keep her; and, moreover, I will maintain my right to her against you in combat!'

When Guigemar heard this he called his men to horse and rode away with a challenge, though it grieved him sorely to leave his lady.

All the knights in the town, who had come thither to the tournament, followed Guigemar, pledging him their faith to go whithersoever he went – 'twere great shame if any failed him now. That same night they arrived at the castle which Meriadus was attacking. The lord of this was joyful and glad to harbour them; for he knew well that .with the aid of Guigemar his war was ended.

On the morrow they rose betimes, armed themselves in their lodgings, and issued forth from the town with great clangor, Guigemar at their head. Finding that the castle was too strong to be taken by assault, they laid siege to it, for Guigemar would not turn hence until he had captured it. His friends and followers grew ever in strength until at last they reduced those within by hunger, seized and destroyed the castle, and slew its lord.

And with great joy Guigemar took away his lady, for now is all his woe overpassed.

Of this story which you have heard was made the *Lay of Guigemar*. Folk tell it to the harp and to the rote; and the music of it is sweet to hear.

THE ASH TREE

I WILL TELL YOU the *Lay of the Ash Tree*, even as I know it.

Long ago there dwelt in Brittany two knights hard by each other. They were rich and of good estate, worthy and valiant men; kinsmen too they were and of one land. Each had married him a wife.

One of the dames in due course had twin-sons; whereupon her lord was blithe and merry, and for the joy that he had, sent his good neighbour tidings how his wife had two sons, one of whom should be sent him for fosterage, and should bear his name.

Now as this other knight was sitting at dinner, lo! the messenger entered, and kneeling before the daïs, delivered his tidings, for which the lord thanked God, and gave the bearer a good horse.

But the lady laughed as she sat by her husband at table, for she was false and proud-hearted, evil of speech and full of envy. Right foolishly she talked, saying in the presence of all her folk:

'So help me God, I marvel that this good man has been so ill-advised as to send my lord word of his dishonour, in that his wife has had twin-children. They are alike put to shame in this thing, for we know well that it never could befall a virtuous woman; it never was, nor ever shall come to pass!'

Her husband, who was watching her, chid her sternly. 'Wife,' he said, 'let be! You should not speak thus, for truly the lady has always been of good report.'

These words were marked by the folk of the household, and were soon spread abroad through all Brittany, so that the foolish dame was much despised, especially by women, both rich and poor. And afterwards grievous misfortune came upon her because of her folly!

The messenger told his lord what had happened; and he, hearing the tale, was sorrowful and knew not what to do. But he began to hate his good wife and sorely to mistrust her, and so kept her in close durance, although she was in no wise to blame.

Yet within the year was she avenged. This same neighbour who had spoken so ill, herself became the mother of twin-daughters. And because of this she had bitter grief, and bewailed herself, saying: 'Alas! what shall I do? Now verily am I put to shame, and never again shall be held in honour! My husband and my kinsmen – surely they will lose all faith in me when they hear of this mischance! I judged myself in speaking ill against all women, when I said that it never happened – nor have we seen such a thing! – that a virtuous woman might have twin-children. Yet have I two, and, I trow, no worse thing could befall me! He who slanders another, and speaks falsely against him, knows not what may hang over his own head; hence, one should speak of his neighbour only when he can praise. To save my good name I must put to death one of the babes, for it is easier to do penance before God than to be dishonoured in the sight of men!'

Her chamberwomen consoled her as they could, but declared that they should not permit this deed; for murder is no light thing! But one of them, a maiden of gentle birth, whom for a long time the lady had fostered and cherished with all tenderness, was much distressed to behold her grief and to hear her sorrowful lamentations, and came to comfort her.

'Lady,' she said, 'this is to no purpose; you will do better to make an end of your sorrowing. Give me one of the babes – so! To spare you shame I will take it away, and you shall never see it again. I will bear it all safe and sound to a monastery, and leave it where some good man may find it, and, please God, take it to foster.'

The lady hearing this, was joyful, and promised the damsel fair guerdon for doing her this service. They wrapped the gentle babe in a piece of fine linen, and put over this a spangled silk of wondrous beauty that the knight had brought back from Constantinople when he was there. Moreover, with a strip of her girdle, the lady tied to the child's arm a heavy ring, as much as an ounce of pure gold, the circlet being engraved and set with a ruby. This she did that whosoever found the little maid might know that she was born of high folk.

Then the damsel took the babe and went forth from the chamber. And when the darkness of evening had fallen, she set out from the village by a highway leading into the forest. Straight through the wood she went, never once leaving the highway, and came out safely with the child. Presently she heard far off to the right the barking of dogs and crowing of cocks; and in this direction she turned her steps, hoping to come upon a village. And after a while she entered one that seemed fair and thriving, in which she found an exceeding rich and well-appointed abbey, where, as I know well, lived nuns and the abbess who ruled them.

When the maiden saw the monastery, with its towers, its walls, and its belfry, she went quickly up to the gate, and laying down before it the child that she carried, made her orison:

'O God,' she prayed, 'by Thy Holy Name, Lord, if it be Thy will, save this little one from death!'

When she had ended her prayer, she looked behind her and saw a spreading ash tree, dense with boughs and branches, which had been planted there for shade. So, taking the child in her arms again, she came running thither and put the little one within the tree where the trunk split into four forks. Then, commending it to God, she returned and told her lady what she had done.

In this abbey was a porter, whose duty it was to open the outer gate of the monastery when folk came to hear the service. On this self-same night he rose betimes, lighted candles and lamps, and rang the bells. When he opened the gate he spied the garments on the ash tree, and supposed that some one had taken them in theft and had hidden them there – he had no thought of anything else.

He went thither faster than he well could, reached up and found the child; whereupon not having the heart to leave it there, he thanked God and carried it home to his dwelling.

With him lived his daughter, a widow, who had a little babe in the cradle, still unweaned. Her the good man roused, calling:

Come, daughter, rise now, and light fire and candle. I have brought in a child that I found outside in the ash tree. Give it some milk, warm it, and bathe it!'

She at his bidding lighted the fire and took the little one, warmed it, bathed it, and gave it milk. And when they had looked upon the rich and beautiful mantle, and had found the ring on the little arm, they knew well enough that the child was born of great folk.

On the morrow, after the service, when the abbess came out of the church, the porter went up to tell her of the babe that he had found; and was straightway commanded to bring it to her, just as it was when he found it.

The porter went home and took the babe gladly to show his lady. And when she had looked at it hard for a while, she said that she would take it to foster and give out that it was her niece. Moreover, she forbade the porter to tell how the matter really stood.

So the abbess herself reared the child, and called her, because she had been found in the ash tree, *Le Fraisne*; and by this name she came to be known.

Thus for a long time she remained concealed, being nurtured within the monastery-close as the niece of the abbess. When she was seven years old, she was a fair maid and tall for her age; and as soon as she was old enough to understand reason, the abbess, who loved her with all tenderness and clad her richly, had her well instructed. By the time that she came to the age of beauty, she was the fairest damsel and the most courteous in all Brittany. So lovely was she and so mannerly, both in bearing and in speech, that all who beheld her loved her and praised marvellously; and great lords came to the abbess, asking leave to see and to speak with her fair niece.

Now there was a certain lord of Dol, named Gurun – the best seigneur indeed that ever was or will be – who heard tell of this maiden. Straightway he loved her; and as he was going to a tournament, came back by way of the abbey. And when the abbess at his request brought the maiden before him, he found her so beautiful and so well taught, so discreet and gracious, and endued with virtues, that unless he might win her love he would hold himself most wretched of men. Yet he was without counsel and knew no way, for if he came there often the abbess would soon understand, and would make an end of his seeing the damsel.

But presently he devised a thing: to endow the abbey with so much of his land that it would be the richer ever after. Therefore to win him friendship and leave to enter there and sojourn at his will, he gave largely of his possessions. I warrant you he had other reason than the salvation of his soul!

Thus he went many times to the convent and talked with the maiden until at length, by prayers and promises, he won her love. And when he was assured of this, he said to her one day:

'Sweet, now this is how it is: since you have made me your lover, it is better that you should come away with me altogether. I say what I think, you know, that if your aunt should discover this she would be sorely distressed. So, if you take my counsel, you will come away with me. Certes! I will never be false to you, but will care for you most tenderly!'

She loved him so clearly that she granted what he pleased, and so went away with him to his castle. But perhaps it may yet be well with her, for she took with her the silken mantle and the ring, which the abbess had given her. Indeed the damsel knew all that had happened from the time that she was put away: how she was cradled in the ash tree, how the mantle and the ring, and nothing else, had been left with her by those who put her away, and how the abbess had fostered her as a niece. Knowing this story she had kept these things carefully locked in a coffer, and was unwilling to leave them behind.

Now this knight with whom she fled loved her most tenderly; and among all his liegemen and servants there was not one, great or small, who did not cherish her and honour her for her gentlehood.

She was with him a long time, until at last the knights who had fief of him, thought ill of it, and told him again and again that he should put her away and espouse a lady of noble birth. They would rejoice if he had heir to hold after him his land and his heritage; indeed, he wronged them too greatly in that, for love of his mistress, he had neither wife nor child. Nay, more, they would not hold him as seigneur, nor be willing to do him service, unless he yielded to their demand. And at last the knight consented, upon their urging, to take wife.

Then further they bethought them who she should be, and said:

'Sire, there is a nobleman dwelling hard by you who has spoken with us on this matter. He has but one daughter and no other heir; hence with her you may gain much land. The maiden, who is the fairest in all this realm, is called *La Coldre*; and so for *Le Fraisne* whom you give up you shall have in recompense *La Coldre*; for the barren Ash, the Hazel with its pleasant nuts. We shall speak fair for the maiden, and, please God, shall bring her to you.'

Accordingly they arranged this marriage, and ratified it on all sides. Alas! what an ill chance that these worthy men knew not that the damsels were twinsisters! *Le Fraisne* was put away that her lover might marry her sister.

When she heard of this she gave no sign of anger, but continued to serve her lord in all kindness and to honour his folk. But the knights of the household, nay even the squires and the pages, grieved marvellously because they must lose her.

On the day agreed upon for the wedding, the knight summoned his friends, and among them the Archbishop of Dol, who held fief of him.

With the bride came her mother, much fearing that her daughter would be abused to the knight by the damsel whom he loved so well; hence she was minded to counsel him that he dismiss her from his household, and rid himself of her by wedding her to some honest man.

The marriage feast was held with great splendour and rejoicing. All the while, the damsel was in the chamber, yet never once, for anything that she saw, made sign of grief nor even of vexation. Sweetly and right deftly she served before the lady, so that all the guests, men and women alike, held her demeanour in great marvel. Even her mother, who watched her closely, commended her in her own heart, and loved her, thinking that if she had known what manner of woman this was, not for her own daughter's sake would she have undone her by parting her from her lord.

At night the damsel withdrew to prepare the bed for the bride. Putting aside her mantle, she called the chamberlains, and showed them the way that her lord wished it – for often enough had she seen it. When they had made it ready, they placed upon it as coverlet an old *bofu*-cloth. But the maiden was vexed because it seemed to her no longer good enough, so she went to her coffer and took out her silken mantle to lay upon the bed. For her lord's honour she did this, since the archbishop, according to his duty, would come into the chamber to bless the newly-wedded, and to sign them with the cross.

When the chamber was empty, the dame entered to bring the bride to bed, and bade disrobe her. Presently she beheld the silk coverlet on the bed, the fairest she had ever looked upon, save that alone which she had wrapped about her little daughter whom she had put away. And as she remembered all this, her heart trembled. She called to her the chamberlain, and said:

'Tell me, by thy faith, where this good silk was found!'

'Lady,' he said, 'you shall know at once. The damsel brought it to throw over the coverlet, because this seemed to her not good enough. I trow that the silk is hers.'

Thereupon the lady sent for her, and she came in, humbly laying aside her mantle.

'Dear child,' said the lady, 'hide nothing from me. Where did you get this mantle of fair silk? How did it come to you? Who gave it you? Now tell me who gave it you!'

The damsel answered: 'Lady, the abbess, my aunt, who fostered me, gave it me, bidding me keep it well, for this and a ring were left with me by those who sent me away to be nurtured.'

'Dear, may I see the ring?'

'Yes, lady, right willingly.'

And when she had brought the ring, the lady looked at it long, knowing it as she had known the mantle; and when she had heard the whole story, being assured beyond doubt that Le Fraisne was her daughter, she hid it no longer, but said:

'Thou art my child, dear heart!'

For sheer pity she fell back in a swoon; but presently recovered and sent in all haste for her husband.

He came thither greatly amazed; and no sooner had he entered the room than she threw herself at his feet, and kissing them often, sought pardon for her misdeed. But he could not understand what she meant.

'Wife,' he said, 'what is this you are saying? Between us can be no such word as *pardon* but since you will have it so, you are forgiven. Tell me what you would.'

'My lord, now that you have forgiven me, I will tell you, if you will listen. Long ago, through great discourtesy, I spoke foolishly about my neighbour, and slandered her because of her twin-children; but all the while I was speaking to my own hurt, for afterwards, of a truth, I had twin-daughters. But I concealed one of them, sending her away to a monastery, and with her your silk mantle and the ring that you gave me when you first spoke with me. And now I may not hide it longer, for I have found them here, and thereby have discovered our daughter, whom through my folly I had lost. This is she, this damsel who is so modest and wise and fair that she was loved by the knight who has wedded her sister.'

The baron answered: 'This rejoices my heart; never before have I been so glad! Verily God has been merciful to us in restoring our daughter before we should have doubled our sins against her. My child, come to me!'

And the damsel, hearing all this, was exceeding glad.

Her father would not delay longer, but went himself to his son-in-law and the archbishop, and brought them thither, repeating to them this strange chance. And when the young knight heard it, he was more glad than ever before in his life. But the archbishop counselled that they let be for that night, and on the morrow he would annul the marriage and wed Gurun to his love. They accorded that it should be thus.

On the morrow this was done; and the damsel's father with right good will gave her away as bride, and with her a share in his heritage. And he, with his wife and daughter, remained at the wedding as long as it lasted.

They made anew a banquet so splendid that even a rich man might well grudge what they spent upon it. For their joy in their daughter, fair and stately as a queen, whom they had so marvellously recovered, they had a wondrous merrymaking.

Presently they returned to their domain with their daughter, *La Coldre;* and afterwards in their own realm she was well bestowed in marriage.

When this adventure came to be known, the *Lay of the Ash Tree* was made thereof, and so named for the lady's sake.

THE TWO LOVERS

ONG AGO THERE befell in Normandy an adventure often told, of two young lovers, who through their love died. Of this the Britons made a lay called *Les Dous Amanz*.

It is well known that in Neustria, which we call Normandy, there is a great mountain marvellous high, on which is the tomb of these lovers. Near this mountain on one side, a king who was lord of the Pistreis, with good judgement and care, had built him a city, and from his folk called it Pitres. There is still a town of that name in this place; and indeed the whole country, as we know well, is called the Vale of Pitres.

Now this king had a daughter, a fair and gentle maiden. She was his only child, and dearly he loved and cherished her. Though she was sought in marriage by great lords, who gladly would have had her to wife, the king was so loth to part with her that he would never consent. Since the death of his queen she had been his only comfort, and he must needs have her near him day and night. This too, although many turned it to ill, and his own men blamed him for it.

When he heard what folk were saying, he was sorely perplexed and troubled; and began to wonder how he might free himself from this seeking of his daughter. Accordingly, he made proclamation far and wide, saying:

Whoso would marry his daughter, let him know of a truth one thing: it had been decreed that he must first carry her in his arms, without pausing for rest, to the top of the mountain near the city.

When these tidings were known and spread through the country, many knights essayed the feat, but could bring it to no ending. Some indeed by using all their strength could carry her half-way up the mountain, but no further; hence there must let be. A long time she remained unbestowed, in that no one came to seek her.

There was in this land a goodly and noble squire, the son of a count, who above all others set himself to win glory by his prowess. He was familiar at the king's court, since he often sojourned there; and he came to love the princess. Again and again he besought her to show him favour and grant him her love, and inasmuch as he was brave and courteous, and much praised of the king, she assented thereto; and he thanked her in all humility for her grace.

Often times they spoke together, and loved each other well, yet must hide it as far as they could from all eyes. Grievous as this was, the lad bethought him that it was better to endure this constraint than hasten over much and lose his lady. Yet was he so sore distraught for love, this fair and goodly squire, that on a time he came to his love, and with sorrowful plaint begged her distressfully to flee with him, since he could no longer bear this woe. He knew well that if he asked her of her father, he might never win her, unless he could carry her in his arms to the top of the mountain.

The damsel answered him, saying: 'Friend, I know well that it would not avail you to attempt this feat – you are not strong enough. And if I were to flee with you, my father would be so grieved and angry that it were torment for him to live; and certainly I love him too well to distress him in this way. We must find other counsel, for to this I will not hearken. But I have a kinswoman in Salerno, a rich dame and of great rent, who has been there more than thirty years, and practised the art of medicine until she is wise in potions and cunning in herbs and roots. If you go to her with a letter from me, and show her all your state, she will consider how she may help you, and will give you such draughts and such electuaries that they will comfort you and give you strength. Then return to this land and seek me of my father, even though he deem you but a child and tell you the condition, that only by carrying me up the mountain without pause for rest may a man win me; and even though he hold with all courtesy that it may not be otherwise.'

The squire, rejoicing greatly in his lady's counsel, thanked her and asked her leave to depart to his own domain. There he speedily provided himself with rich robes and deniers, with palfreys and pack-horses; and taking with him the most trusty of his men, went to Salerno to speak with his lady's kinswoman.

He gave her his letter, and when she had read it from beginning to end, she kept him with her until she knew all his state. Then she strengthened him with potions, and further gave him a draught such that he should never be so for-worn by travail, nor so weary nor so oppressed that it would not refresh his whole body, alike his veins and his bones, and give him his full strength as soon as he had drunk it.

Thereupon the squire, all joyous and glad at heart, returned to his own land, having the draught with him in a phial. He went straightway to the king to ask for his daughter, that he might take her and carry her up the mountain.

The king did not refuse him, though he thought it great folly, in that he was but a lad, and many good men, strong and wise, had essayed this feat and could bring it to no ending. But he appointed a time, and summoned his liegemen and his friends, and all whom he could get together. For the sake of the princess and of the lad who undertook the adventure of carrying her up the mountain, they came thither from all parts.

On the day of their assembling, the squire was there first of all, by no means forgetting his draught. Then among the great folk gathered in the meadow along the Seine, the king led forth his daughter, who, to help her lover, had made herself as thin as possible by fasting, and was now clad in smock alone.

The squire took her in his arms; and knowing well that she would not betray him, gave her the little phial with all the draught, to carry in her hand. Yet I fear that it will not avail him, for in him is no measure at all!

He set out with her at a great pace, and climbed the mountain to half its height. And for the joy that he had in her, he was all unmindful of the drink; but she felt that he was wearying.

'Dear,' she said, 'drink now. I know well that you are weary, and thus will you regain your strength.'

The squire answered, 'Sweet, I feel my heart all strong. By no means would I stop long enough to drink, while I am able to go three steps. Yonder folk would cry out upon us and would confuse me with their noise, so that they might easily hinder me. I will not stop here.'

When he had climbed two-thirds of the way, he could scarcely stand. Again and again the maiden implored him, 'Love, drink the potion!' But now he would not hear her or heed, as he struggled on in great anguish. He came at last to the mountain-top, but so for-spent that he fell there and rose not again, for the heart failed in his breast.

The maiden, as she looked upon her lover, deemed him in swoon; and falling on her knees by his side, strove to give him the drink. But he could not speak to her, and died as I have told you.

She mourned him with much shrill crying; and presently cast from her and shattered the vessel with its draught. The mountain was well sprinkled with it, so that in summer all the land thereabouts was the richer for it. There is many a good herb found to-day that had its root in the potion.

But to speak again of the maiden. Never in all her life was she so sorrowful as now in losing her lover. She threw herself upon him, clasped him in her arms and held him close, often kissing his eyes and mouth, until her grief touched her to the quick; and there she died, this damsel so gentle and wise and fair.

The king and his men awaited them long; and perceiving at last that they would not come, went up and found them thus. Thereupon the king fell to the earth in a swoon, and when he could speak made exceeding great dole; and so did the folk from other lands.

Three days they kept the twain above earth, then placed them in a marble tomb, by the counsel of all buried them on the mountain; and presently went their ways.

The story of the two young lovers, from whom the mountain is called *La Cote des Deux Amants*, befell even as I have told you; and the Britons made it into a lay.

YONEC

INCE I HAVE undertaken these lays, however great the labour, I will not leave them unfinished; but will tell in rhyme all the adventures that I know. And now it is in my thought to tell you of Yonec, whose son he was, and how his father, Muldumarec, first came to his mother.

In Britain long ago there dwelt a rich man and very ancient, who was provost of Caruënt, and lord of the land round about. This city is on the river Duëlas, where in ancient times folk crossed by a ferry.

Now this old man was heavy-burdened with years, yet since he had a goodly heritage, he took wife for the sake of children to hold his land after him. The lady who was bestowed upon him was of high rank, and moreover discreet and gentle and passing fair, so that for her beauty he loved her well. What need of more words? As far as Lincoln, nay, even to Iceland, there was none so lovely as she! It was a great sin to marry her to this lord, for in that she was so fair and sweet, he thought only how to guard her well, and shut her up in a great paved chamber in his tower.

And the better to keep watch over her, he placed there also his sister, an ancient dame, and widowed of her husband. There were other women as well, I trow, in a chamber by themselves; but the lady might not speak to them unless the aged dame gave her leave.

In this wise, even though they had no child, he kept her more than seven years, so that she never once went out of the tower to see either kinsman or friend. And when her lord went there to sleep, he would not allow usher or chamberlain to enter the room or to light candle for him. Accordingly, the lady was in such deep sadness that with her tears and sighs and lamentations she lost her beauty, even as one who has no care for it; and wished only that death would come quickly and take her.

One morning in the beginning of April when birds sing all the while, this lord arose early and went to walk in the woods, bidding the old woman to rise at once and make fast the door after him. She did as he commanded, then passed into another room with her psalter in her hand, to read verses therein.

The lady, wide-awake and in tears, watched the clear light of the sun; and when she perceived that the old woman was gone forth from the chamber, sighed and fell into bitter weeping, bewailing herself and saying:

'Alas, would that I had never been born! Hard is my fate, in that I am shut up in this tower, and may never leave it until I die. This jealous old man, of whom is he afraid, that he keeps me in such close prison? Indeed, he is foolish and cowardly in thus fearing ever to be betrayed. I may not even go to church to hear God's service! If only I might talk with other people, and go with my husband when he takes his pleasure,

I would show him fair looks, nor have any wish to be false to him. Accursed be my kinsmen and the others who bestowed me upon this Jealous, and wedded me to him, for now am I always pulling and dragging at a strong cord! He will never die! When he was baptized, he was plunged into the river of hell, so that his nerves and his veins are all hard, and filled with the sap of life!

'Yet I have heard tell sometimes, how in this land long ago folk found ways to rescue the unhappy. Knights could have sweet and fair maidens, if they would; and ladies might have goodly and courteous lovers, strong men and valiant, and this without any blame whatsoever, for they were invisible to all save themselves. If this may be, and has been, if it ever befell any one, may the Almighty God grant me my heart's desire!'

When she had ended her plaint, she beheld the shadow of a great bird athwart a narrow window – and knew not what this might be. It flew into the room, a falcon seemingly of five or six moultings, and crouched before her. And when it had been there a little while, even as she watched it, it changed into a fair and gentle knight.

Now the lady held this for a great marvel. Her blood curdled and froze, and she covered her head for affright. But the stranger was full of courtesy, and at once reassured her.

[57]

'Lady,' he said, 'have no fear. The falcon is a gentle bird, even though the mystery of his coming be dark to you. Look to it that you be unobserved, then take me for your lover. To this very end am I come hither, for I have loved you long, and in my heart desired you. I have never loved woman save you alone, nor will I love any other; but I could not leave my own country to come to you until you wished for me. Now I may be your lover!'

The lady took courage, uncovered her head and an-swered the knight, saying that she would have him for her friend on one condition. If he believed in God, she was content that there be love between them, for he was the fairest knight that she had looked upon in all her life, nor would she ever again see one so goodly.

'Lady, you speak well,' said he. 'In no wise would I that you have any cause to doubt or to suspect me. I believe verily in the Creator, who delivered us from the woe of death, wherein our father, Adam, placed us, because of the bitter apple. He is, and was always, and shall be, life and light to sinners. If still you doubt me in this, send for your chaplain, saying that illness has come upon you, and you would take the Sacra-ment, which God has ordained in the world to save sinners. I will make myself like you in appearance, and thus will receive the Body of the Lord God; and I will tell you all my creed, so that you shall be in no manner of doubt.'

She answered that he spoke well. Thereupon he sat down beside her; but in no wise would he as yet kiss her or embrace.

Presently the old woman returned, and finding the lady awake, said that it was time to arise, and that she would fetch her garments. But the lady answered that she was ill, and that the chaplain should be sent for, to come at once, for she was in great fear of death.

The aged dame said: 'Well, you must bear it. My lord has gone into the woods, and none may enter here within save myself.'

Then indeed the lady was greatly affrighted, and made pretence of swooning. And when the other saw this, she was so dismayed that she undid the chamber door and asked for the priest. He came thither as quickly as he could, bearing *corpus domini*; and when the knight had received it, and had drunk wine from the chalice, the chaplain went away again, and the old woman made fast the door.

Never have I seen so fair a couple as this lady and her lover. But presently when they had been happy together awhile, and had talked to their heart's content, the knight took leave, for he must needs return to his own country. Most sweetly she prayed him to come back to her often.

'Lady,' he said, 'whenever you please. Not an hour shall pass by without my coming, if only you take heed, so that neither of us be suspected. This old woman will watch day and night to betray us; and when she perceives our love, will bear word of it to her lord. If it should happen as I say, and we should be betrayed, I could never escape, but should have to die here.'

With these words he departed; but left the lady well content. On the morrow she arose quite recovered; and the whole week was full of joy to her. She tended her body with such great care that she soon regained her beauty. Now is she happier in biding at home than in going to any mirth whatsoever. Often she longs to see her friend and to be happy with him, and as soon as her husband is departed, night and day, early and late, she has him at her will. May God grant them long to joy!

For the great gladness that she had in seeing her lover so often, her whole appearance was changed. Hence, her husband, who was right crafty, perceived in his heart that things were otherwise than usual; and mistrusting his sister somewhat, took her to task one day, saying that he marvelled that his wife should so apparel herself, and asking what this meant.

The old dame answered that she knew not, for none might speak with her, nor had she lover or friend. Only one thing had she herself perceived, that the lady remained alone more willingly than she was wont to do.

Thereupon the lord made answer:

'By my faith,' he said, 'I believe it well. But now it behoves you to do something. In the morning when I have risen and you have made fast the door, pretend to go away and leave her lying alone. But stay in some secret place, and watch and mark what this may be, and whence it comes that she has in herself such great joy.'

And with this counsel they parted.

Alas, in evil plight were they who were thus plotted against, to their betrayal and their undoing!

Three days later, I have heard tell, the lord feigned to go away, saying to his wife that the king had sent for him by letter, but that he would soon return. Then he went out of the chamber, and made fast the door; and the old dame arose and hid behind a curtain, in the hope of seeing and hearing what she was eager to know.

The lady lay still but not asleep, for she was longing for her friend. He came at once, nor delayed even a moment. Great was their joy together, as appeared both by words and by looks, until it was time to arise, when he must needs depart.

The old woman watched well, noting how he came and went, though when she saw him now man and now falcon, she was in great fear.

Upon the return of the lord, who had not journeyed far, she revealed to him the truth concerning the knight. He fell into deep study, and speedily devised a trap whereby to slay the stranger. He had great prongs of iron forged, and their edges sharpened in front until they were keener than any razor under heaven. When he had them all finished, and pointed in different directions, he placed them, well serried and firmly fixed, on the window by which the knight entered when he visited the lady. God! that he knew nothing or the treachery planned by these wretches!

On the morrow morning, the lord arose at dawn, saying that he would go a-hunting. The old woman helped him forth, then lay down again to sleep until it should be full day.

The lady was awake and waiting for him whom she loved dearly; and said to herself that now was a time when he might well come and be with her.

As soon as she had wished for him, he came with no delay, flying into the window; but the prongs were in the way, and one of them pierced his body, so that the red blood gushed out.

When he knew that he was wounded to the death, he freed himself from the iron, and entering alighted in front of the lady, on the bed, so that all the coverings were blood-stained. Thereupon she shrank back in horror at the sight. He said to her:

'My sweet friend, for love of you I am losing my life. Surely I have told you that your changed looks would undo us.'

Hearing this, she fell back in a swoon; and remained thus while one might run a league.

Sweetly he strove to comfort her, saying that grief was of no avail; let her think of the child that was to come, the strong and valiant son, who would be her comfort; and he, who should be called Yonec, would avenge them both by slaying their enemy.

But the knight could stay no longer, for his wound bled unceasingly; and so departed with great sorrow and anguish.

Yet she followed him, crying aloud, and passed through the window after him – 'tis a marvel that she was not killed, for there where she escaped was a fall of twenty feet.

Clad in her smock only, she followed the track of the knight's blood along the windings and wanderings of the road until it brought her finally to a cave, where the entrance was all wet with the blood. She could see nothing beyond, yet knowing well that her lover had passed through here, she followed as quickly as she could, held her way straight on through the darkness, until she came out of the cave into a most fair meadow.

Here she found the grass all bloodstained, and shuddering followed the track across the field, until she perceived close at hand a city, quite encompassed with a wall. Every house there within, alike hall and tower, was made entirely of silver – wondrous were all the buildings! About the city were moorlands and forests and parks, and on the side where the donjon was, flowed a stream large enough for the landing of boats; indeed, more than three hundred masts could be seen there.

The lower part of the gate was unfastened, and the lady entered the city; and still following the blood-tracks, passed through the streets to the castle.

And all the way none spoke to her; nay, she did not even see man or woman in that place.

She came at last to the palace, with its pavement all blood-stained, and entered a fair chamber wherein she found a sleeping knight. But she did not know him, so passed on into another room still more spacious, wherein was only a bed and upon it a knight asleep.

She went her way yet further, and in the third chamber found her lover's bed. Its feet were made of the finest gold; the coverlets I know not how to praise; the candlesticks, in which tapers were burning night and day, were worth all the gold of a city.

She knew the knight as soon as she had beheld him, went forward all in affright and fell swooning by his side. He raised her up as one who loved her dearly, often calling himself wretched; and when she was recovered, comforted her with all tenderness.

'Dear love, for God's sake, I pray you, go hence; flee from here! As soon as I shall die, this very day, here within shall be so great mourning, that if you were found here, you would be most harshly dealt with, for my people will know that they have lost me through my love of you. It is for your sake that I am anxious and distressed!'

The lady answered, 'Dear, I would rather die here with you than suffer torture from my husband; if I return to him he will surely kill me!'

But the knight reassured her by giving her a little ring and showing how, as long as she should keep this, her husband would not remember any thing that had happened, nor in any wise deal with her harshly. He also put into her charge his sword, adjuring her to let no man have it, but to keep it well for her son. And when he should be grown and tall, and a brave and strong knight, she would go with him and her husband to a feast, and on the way they would come to an abbey, wherein by the side of a tomb they would hear told again the story of his death, how he was slain basely. 'Then give him the sword! Tell him how he was born and who was his father; soon enough they shall see what he will make of it!'

When he had revealed everything to her, he gave her a costly robe to put on; then made her hurry away.

She departed, bearing with her the ring and the sword, in which she found comfort. And after she had left the city, she had not gone half a league before she heard the tolling of bells and in the castle the sound of dole for the dying lord.

And when she knew that he was dead, in her grief she swooned as many as four times. But at last she was able to hold her way to the cave, entered in and passed beyond – so returned to her own country.

She lived with her husband many a day and many a year; but he never blamed her for this deed, nor spoke ill to her, nor mocked at her.

In due time her son was born and was called Yonec. He was tenderly nurtured and carefully reared, so that in all the realm was no lad so fair, so strong, so brave, so generous, so open-handed. When he came of age, he was dubbed knight; and – hearken now to what befel in this very year!

After the custom of the country, the old lord was summoned with his friends to the feast of St. Aaron, which was celebrated in Cærleon and many other cities. So he went thither with his wife and son in splendid array. Although they set out for Cærleon, they did not know the way thither, so took with them a young lad as guide. And presently they came to a castled town, the fairest in all that age, in which was an abbey for religious men. Their guide brought them there for harbourage; and in the abbot's own chamber they were well served and held in honour.

On the morrow they went to hear mass, then would have departed; but the abbot went to them and prayed them earnestly to tarry, and he would show them his dormitory, his chapter-house and his refectory. Since they had been so well harboured there, the lord was not loth to grant this.

On this same day after dinner, they went to the monastic buildings, and first of all to the chapter house. Here they found a great tomb covered with a spangled silk all bordered with costly gold-embroidery. At the head, at the feet, and at the sides, were twenty lighted tapers, in candlesticks of fine gold. The censers, with which for great honour they clouded that tomb all day long, were made of amethyst.

The strangers asked the folk of the land whose this tomb was and what manner of man lay there. And they began to weep, and said sorrowfully that he was the best and strongest knight, the bravest, fairest, and best-beloved, that was born in that age.

'Of this land he was king – and never was any so courteous! At Cæruënt he was beguiled and slain for love of a lady. Never since then have we had a liege-lord, but have been waiting many a day for a son who should be born of that lady, as he told us, and commanded us to do.'

When the lady heard these words, with a loud voice she called her son, saying:

'Fair son, you have heard how God has led us thither! He who lies there is your father, slain treacherously by this old man! Now I yield and deliver to you his sword, for long enough have I kept it!'

In the presence of all she showed whose son he was, telling how the knight had been wont to come and visit her, and how her husband had entrapped him. And when she had told the whole story, she fell swooning on the grave, and never spoke again; and thus passed away.

When her son saw that she had died, with the sword that had been his father's, he struck off the old man's head, and so avenged both his parents.

When it was known through the city what had befallen, they took the lady and placed her with great honour in her lover's tomb. May God grant them sweet mercy!

Yonec they made their liege-lord before they departed from that place.

Some who heard this adventure told, long afterwards made of it a lay, to show the pain and the sorrow that these suffered for love's sake.

THE NIGHTINGALE

WILL TELL YOU an adventure where-
of the Britons made a lay. This is called
Laustic, I understand, in their country, but
russignol in French, and in plain English, *nihtegale*. In
the country near St. Malo was a well-known village,
in which two knights, whose bounty gave it fair name,
had their homes and their parks.

The one was married to a lady who was wise, courteous and debonair; and marvellously he doted upon
her, as often comes to pass in such a case.

The other was a bachelor who was known among
his fellows for his prowess and his great courage. So
eagerly did he seek honour that he was often at tour-
naments, spent freely, and gave largesse abundantly of
what he had.

Now he came to love his neighbour's wife, and by
dint of his entreaties and prayers brought it about
that she loved him above all things. This was partly
for his deserts, partly because of the good which she
heard said of him, and partly because he was ever at
hand.

They loved each other well, yet wisely, so guarding
their secret that they were not observed, nor discovered, nor even mistrusted. It was easy for them to do
this, since their dwellings, both halls and donjons,
stood side by side, with no bar or barrier between
them save a high wall of grey stone.

When the lady stood at the window of the chamber in which she slept, she could speak with her lover, and he from his side with her; and they could exchange gifts by throwing or by tossing.

They had nothing at all to grieve them; but were quite happy, except that they might not meet as they would, for the lady was straitly guarded when her lord was in the country. But at least none might hinder them from going to the window, either by day or by night, and there gazing upon each other and talking together.

A long time they were in love, until at length came summer, when wood and meadow were green once more, and copses were a-flower. The little birds right sweetly trilled their joy at the tips of the blossoms, 'Tis no marvel that he who has love-longing in his heart should give heed thereto; and so, I tell you truly, it was with this knight and this lady, both in words and in glances.

The nights when the moon shone clear, the lady rose from her husband's side, as he lay asleep, and wrapping herself in her mantle, went to stand at the window, for she knew that her lover would be there, since like herself he waked most of the night for love-longing. It was joy to them to see each other, since they might have no more.

So often she arose and stood there that at last her husband was vexed, and often asked her why she arose and whither she went.

'My lord,' she answered, 'there is no joy in this world like that of hearing the nightingale sing, and this is why I come to stand here. So sweetly have I heard him trill at night, and such great pleasure has his song given me, that I long for it until I cannot close an eye in sleep!'

When her husband heard this, he laughed for sheer vexation and ill-humour; and bethought him that he would ensnare the nightingale.

Accordingly, there was no lad in his household who did not make trap or toil or net, to place in the copse. In every hazel and every chestnut they put net or lime, until at length they trapped and caught the bird, and brought it alive to their lord.

He, greatly pleased, took it into his wife's chamber, calling out:

'Wife, where are you? Come here and speak to us! I have limed the nightingale for which you have waked so often. Henceforth, you may lie in peace; he shall trouble you no more!'

When the lady heard this, she was both vexed and sorrowful, and demanded the bird of her husband. But he in his passion slew it, wringing its neck with his two hands – a churlish deed! – and flung the body at his wife, so that the front of her smock, a little above the breast, was stained with its blood. Thereupon he left the chamber.

The lady with bitter tears took up the little body, and cursed all who had devised traps and nets to ensnare the nightingale; for they had made an end of her great joy.

'Alas!' she said, 'woe's me! Never again may I rise at night, and stand at the window to see my love. I know of a truth he will deem me false, and for this must I take counsel. I will send him the nightingale at once, and so tell him the whole story.'

In a piece of gold-embroidered samite, duly inscribed, she wrapped the little bird; and calling one of her pages, charged him with the message to her lover.

He went to the knight, and with greetings from his lady told all the message; and delivered to him the nightingale.

When the young lord had heard all the story, he grieved at the mischance; and being neither churlish nor slothful, he had a little casket fashioned, not of iron or steel, but all of fine gold set with rare and costly gems. Then he placed the nightingale within, and had a splendid cover sealed upon it; and everywhere that he went carried the casket about with him.

Not long did their adventure remain unknown; it was put into story, and the Britons made of it a lay which is called *Laustic*.

THE HONEYSUCKLE

T IS MY wish and purpose to tell you truly how, wherefore, and by whom, the *Lay of the Honeysuckle* was made. Many have told it to me and I have also found it in writing, the story of Tristram and of the queen, and of their faithful love that brought manifold woes upon them, and at length upon the same day death itself.

When King Mark heard that Tristram loved the queen, he was bitterly wroth, and banished his nephew from the realm. So the knight went away to his own land, South Wales, where he was born; and tarried there a whole year, knowing no way of return. But at last he was so exceeding sorrowful and distraught for love, that he put himself in peril of death and of undoing; hence, departed from his own land and went straight into Cornwall, where the queen was dwelling. Marvel not at this, for he who loves loyally, is woful and full of despair when he lacks his heart's desire.

Now Tristram would not that any man see him, so he entered all alone into the forest; and came out only at evensong, when it was time to take harbourage. He lodged at night with poor peasant folk, and asked them tidings of the king. From them he heard that all the barons had been summoned to Tintagel where the king, together with the queen, would hold high court at Pentecost, in great mirth and revelry. Upon these tidings Tristram was glad at heart, since the queen could not pass by without his seeing her.

On the day that the king journeyed, Tristram returned to the forest, along the road by which he knew the queen must come. There he cut into a hazel-branch, and stripped it four-square, and when he had made it ready, with his knife he wrote his name. If the queen should see it, she would know the mark as her lover's; and indeed she would watch well for such a thing, since it had happened before that she had met him in this way.

This was the import of the writing that he set upon it: that he had been there long, waiting to catch a glimpse of her, or to know how he might see her, for without her he could not live. The twain of them were like the hazel with the honeysuckle clinging to it; when they are all intertwined and clasped together, they thrive well, but if they be parted, the hazel dies at once, and likewise the honeysuckle.

'Sweet love, so is it with us: nor you without me, nor I without you!'

The queen came riding in cavalcade, and still kept looking a little in front of her, until she saw the hazel, and studying it well, knew all the letters. Thereupon she bade the knights who were attending her to halt, as she would dismount and rest awhile. And they did as she commanded.

Calling to her the maiden Brenguein, who kept good faith with her, she wandered far from her folk; and as she turned aside from the road a little, found in the woods him whom she loved more than any other living thing.

And gladness dwelt with them while he spoke with her at his will, and she showed him all her heart, how she had made accord with the king, who now repented him of banishing his nephew upon an evil charge. But at last they must go their ways, though they wept sorely at the parting; for Tristram must needs return to Wales until his uncle summoned him.

For the joy that he had in his lady, whom he saw by means of the writing on the hazel, Tristram, who was skilled in harping, made a new lay for the remembrance of her words, just as she had spoken them. This is called *Gotelef* in English, and *Chievrefoil* in French. It is truth that I have told you in this lay.

ELIDUC

WILL TELL YOU the story of a most ancient Breton lay, even as I have heard it, and as I believe it to be true.

There dwelt in Brittany a knight called Eliduc, who was noble and courteous, brave and high-hearted – indeed, the most valiant man in the realm. He had married a lady of high lineage, a gentle dame, and of good discretion; and with her he lived a long time in faithful love. But at last it happened that he sought service in a war abroad, and there came to love a damsel called Guilliadun, daughter to a king and queen, and withal the fairest maid in her land. Now Eliduc's wife was called Guildeluëc; and from these two, the lay is named *Guildeluëc and Guilliadun*. It hight *Eliduc* at first, but the name has been changed because the story has to do chiefly with the two ladies. And now I will tell you truly how the adventure befell, whereof the lay was made.

Eliduc was very dear to his lord, the King of Lesser Britain, and rendered unto him such faithful service that whenever the king must needs be absent, he for his prowess was made warden of the land. And still better fortune befell him, for he had the right to hunt in the royal forests, so that no forester dared gainsay him or grudge him at any time. But for envy of his good fortune – as befalls others oftentimes – he was brought into disfavour with his lord, being so accused and slandered that he was banished from court without a hearing, yet knew not wherefore. Again and again he entreated the king to show him justice, and not hearken to false charges, inasmuch as he had served him with good will.

Since the king would hear nothing of it, he must needs depart, so went home, and summoning all his friends, told them of the king's anger – 'twas an ill return for his faithful service! As the peasant says in proverb, when he chides his ploughman, 'Lord's favour is no fief'; so he is wise and prudent who, with all due loyalty to his lord, expends his love upon his good neighbours. The knight said further that he would not remain in the land, but would journey over sea to the realm of Loengre, and there take his pleasure for awhile.

His wife he would leave in his domain, commending her to the charge of his vassals and his friends. In this purpose he remained, and arrayed himself richly, his friends grieving sorely at his departure. He took ten knights with him, and his wife conducted him on the way. When it came to the parting she made exceeding great lamentation; but he assured her that he would keep good faith with her. Thereupon he set forth, held straight on his way until he came to the sea, crossed over and arrived at Totnes,

There were many kings in that land, and they were at strife and war with one another. Among them was one who lived near Exeter, a puissant man but of very great age. He had no son to inherit after him, but only a daughter of an age to wed; and because he would not give her in marriage to his neighbour, this other was making war upon him, and laying waste all his land, had even besieged him in a castle so closely that he had no man who dared make sally against the foe, or engage in mêlée or combat.

Upon hearing of this war, Eliduc decided to go no further, but to remain in the land, and aid as most he might this king who was so wronged and humiliated and hard-pressed. So he sent messengers with letters to say that he had departed from his own country and was come to help the king; but if the king did not wish to retain him, the knight asked for safe-conduct through the realm, that he might go further to seek service.

The king looked kindly upon the messengers, and entertained them well. Calling his constable, he gave commands straightway that an escort be prepared to conduct the knight thither; and that hostels be made ready where the strangers might lodge; and he further set at their disposal as much as they would spend for a month.

The escort was arrayed and sent for Eliduc, and he was received with great honour, for he was passing welcome to the king. He was lodged with a kind and worthy burgess, who gave up to him his fair tapestried chamber. Here Eliduc had a splendid feast served, and invited the needy knights who sojourned in the city. Furthermore, he admonished all his men that none be so forward as to take gift or denier for the first forty days.

On the third day after his arrival, there arose cries in the city that the foe were come and spread throughout the land, and would advance to the very gates and assail the town.

Eliduc hearing the clamour of the frightened folk, armed himself at once, and bade his comrades do likewise. There were forty mounted knights dwelling in that town (though some were wounded and many had been captured); and when they saw Eliduc mounting his horse, all who were able came out of their hostels armed, and went forth from the gate with him, waiting for no summons.

'Sir,' they said, 'we will go with you, and do as you shall do.'

He made answer: 'Gramercy! Is there none among you here who knows a narrow pass meet for an ambush, where we may take them unawares? True, if we await them here, we shall probably fight, but to no advantage, if any knows better counsel.'

And they said: 'Sir, i' faith, in the thicket hard by yonder wood is a narrow road, by which they usually return when they have been plundering, riding unarmed on their palfreys. Again and again they repair thither, thus putting themselves in jeopardy of speedy death, so that they might easily be overcome and put to shame and worsted.'

Eliduc answered: 'Friends, I give you my word that he who does not venture often where he expects to lose shall never win much, nor attain to great renown. Now ye are all the king's men, and should keep good faith with him. Come with me where I shall go, and do as I shall do; and I promise you faithfully that ye shall come to no harm as long as I can aid you. If we gain anything, it will be to our glory to have weakened our foes.'

They took his pledge, and guided him to the forest, where they placed themselves in ambush along the road until the enemy should return. Eliduc commanded in all things, devising and explaining how they should leap out suddenly with loud cries.

As soon as the enemy had come to the narrow pass... Eliduc shouted to his comrades to do worthily. And they gave hard blows, sparing not at all, so that the foe, taken by surprise, were quickly confused and scattered, and in a little while vanquished. Their constable was captured and so many other knights that the squires had much ado to take charge of them. Five-and-twenty were the men of this land, and they took prisoner thirty of those from abroad, and as much armour as they would. 'Twas a marvellous booty; and the knights returned home rejoicing in their exploit.

The king, meanwhile, was on a tower, in great fear for his men, and complaining bitterly of Eliduc, for he supposed, or at least dreaded, that through treason he might have led the knights of that city into danger. And when these came back all in array, and all encumbered with booty and prisoners, so that they were many more at their home-coming than when they went forth, the king did not know them, and so was in doubt and suspense. He gave commands that the gates be closed, and that soldiers be stationed on the walls to shoot, and to hurl darts at them. But all this was needless, for they sent a squire spurring in advance, to tell of the stranger's achievement, how he had vanquished the foe, and how nobly he had borne himself – there never was such a knight! – and how the constable had been captured, and nine-and-twenty others, besides many wounded and many slain.

The king rejoiced marvellously at these tidings, and descended from the tower to meet Eliduc, and to thank him for his good service. He in turn delivered up his prisoners; and divided the booty among the other knights. For his own use he kept only three horses that he liked especially. All his share he distributed and gave out among the prisoners as well as among the other folk.

After this feat of which I have told you, the king greatly loved and cherished him, and for a whole year retained him in his service, and likewise his comrades.

Moreover, after taking his oath, he made him warden of the land.

Now Eliduc was courteous and discreet, a goodly knight, and strong and open-handed; hence, the king's daughter heard him talked of and his virtues recounted. Accordingly, by one of her trusty chamberlains she prayed and commanded him to visit her, that they might have friendly speech together, and become acquainted – indeed, she marvelled greatly that he had not come to her before!

Eliduc answered that he would most gladly go to make her acquaintance. Attended by a single knight, he mounted his horse and rode to her bower, where he sent the chamberlain before, and followed when his coming had been announced.

With sweet courtesy, with gentle manner and with noble bearing, he spoke as one skilled in speech, and thanked the fair lady Guilliadun, in that she had been pleased to summon him to her presence.

She took him by the hand, and they sat down together upon a couch, speaking of many things. She looked at him attentively, studying his face, his stature and his bearing, and said to herself, 'There is no fault in him.' And all at once, as she was praising him in her heart, Love flung his dart at her, bidding her love the knight, whereupon she grew pale and sighed. But she would not put her thought into speech, lest he hold her too lightly.

He tarried there a long while, but at last took leave
– though she granted it unwillingly – and returned to
his hostel. He was right pensive and sadly distraught
for thinking of the fair princess, how she had so sweetly called him, and how she had sighed. His only regret
was that he had been in the land so long, and had not
seen her often. But even as he said this he repented,
minding him of his wife, and how he had promised to
keep good faith with her.

On the other hand, the maid, as soon as she beheld
him, loved him more than any other in the world, and
wished to have him for her lover. All the night she lay
awake, and had neither sleep nor rest. On the morrow morning she arose, and going to a window, called
thither her chamberlain and showed him all her state,
saying:

'By my faith, 'tis ill with me! I am fallen into evil
case! I love the stranger-knight, Eliduc, so that I have
no rest at night, nor can I close my eyes in sleep. If he
would return my love and be my betrothed, I would
do all his will, and he indeed might win great good
therefrom, for he should be king of this land! But if
he will not love me, I must die of grief for very love of
his wisdom and his courtesy!'

When she had said what she would, the chamberlain whom she had called, gave her excellent counsel
– let no man think ill of it!

'Lady,' he said, 'since you love him, send to him and tell him so. It were well, perhaps, to send him a girdle or riband or ring, and if he should accept it gratefully and be joyous at the message, you would be sure of his love. There is no emperor under heaven who, if you would love him, ought not to be right glad!'

And when the damsel had heard this counsel, she answered:

'How shall I know by my gift whether he will love me? Never have I seen knight – whether he loved or hated – who had to be entreated to keep willingly the present one sent him. I should hate bitterly to be a jest to him! Still, one may know somewhat by his manner – make ready, and go!'

'I am all ready,' he said.

'Give him a golden ring, and my girdle. Greet him from me a thousand times!'

The chamberlain turned away, leaving her in such state that she all but called him back; but yet she let him go, and began to lament in this wise:

'Alas! now is my heart captive for a stranger from another land! I know not if he is of high degree, yet if he should go hence suddenly, I should be left mourning. Foolishly have I set my heart's desire, for I never spoke with him save yesterday; and now I have sent to entreat his love. I think that he will blame me – yet if he is gentle, he will show me grace! Now is everything at hazard, and if he cares not for my love, I shall be

[91]

in such sorrow that never again in my life shall I have joy!'

While she was thus bemoaning herself, the chamberlain hastened and came to Eliduc. As had been devised, he greeted the knight according to the maiden's bidding, and gave him the little ring and the girdle. Eliduc thanked him, put the gold ring on his finger, and girt himself with the girdle. But there was no further speech between them, save that the knight proffered gifts, of which the chamberlain would have none.

Returning to his lady, whom he found in her bower, he greeted her on the knight's part and thanked her for her present.

'Come,' she said, 'hide nothing from me. Will he love me with true love?'

'As I think,' he answered. 'The knight is not wanton, but I hold him rather as courteous and discreet in knowing how to hide his heart. I greeted him from you and gave him your gifts, whereupon he girt him himself with your girdle, drawing it close about him, and put the little ring on his finger. Nor said I more to him, nor he to me.'

'Did he not receive it in token of love? If not, I am undone!'

He answered: 'By my faith, I know not; yet, hearken to me, unless he wished you well, he would have none of your gifts.'

'You speak folly!' said she. 'I know well that he does not hate me, for I have never wronged him in aught, save in loving him tenderly; and if for that he hates me, he deserves to die! Never by you, or by any other, will I ask anything of him until I myself speak to him and show how love for him sways me. But I know not whether he remains.'

The chamberlain answered: 'Lady, the king has retained him under oath to serve faithfully for a year; hence, you may have time enough to show him your pleasure.'

When she heard that he would remain, she was exceeding joyful and glad at heart.

She knew nothing of the sorrow that came upon him as soon as he had beheld her, for his only joy was in thinking of her, and he held himself in evil case since he had promised his wife, before he left his domain, to love none but herself. Now is his heart in sore conflict, for he would fain keep his faith, yet in no wise may he doubt that he loves the maiden Guilliadun, so sweet to gaze upon and to speak with, to kiss and to embrace. But he would not seek her love, since it would be dishonourable to his wife, and to the king as well.

For all this, he was so tormented for love that he mounted his horse presently, and rode away with his companions to the castle. But the reason of his going was not so much to speak with the king as to see the maiden, if he might.

Now the king was risen from dinner and entered into his daughter's bower, where he was playing chess with a knight from oversea; and from across the chessboard the princess was watching the game.

As Eliduc came forward, the king showed him great favour, and bade him sit by his side; then, turning to his daughter, he said: 'Damsel, acquaint you with this knight, and show him all honour; for there is none more worthy among five hundred!'

Upon her father's command, the maiden turned joyfully to greet Eliduc; and they sat afar off from the others. Love so overcame them that she dared say no word to him and he could scarce speak to her. Yet he thanked her for her gift, which was to him the dearest thing he had. Thereupon she said that she was glad at heart: she had sent him the ring and the girdle because she loved him so well that she would willingly take him for her husband; and if this might not be, of a truth, never would she have living man! But now, let him show his heart!

'Lady,' he said, 'I thank you for the grace of your love, which fills me with joy! That I stand so high in your favour, makes me glad beyond the telling, yet the future rests not with me, for, although I am bound to remain a year with the king, having given my oath not to depart until his war is ended, after that, I ought to return to my own land without delay, if you will grant me leave.'

The maiden answered: 'My friend, gramercy! So very wise are you and courteous, that ere that time you will have devised what you will do with me. I love and trust you above everything!'

Thus they accorded well, and at that time spake no more. Eliduc returned to his dwelling full of joy; for he had dealt honourably and yet might speak with his lady as often as he would, and between them was the fulness of love's joy.

Accordingly, he entered into the war with such zeal that he seized and took captive the lord who fought against the king, and set free all the land. For his prowess, for his wit and for his largesse, he was praised far and wide, and fair fortune befell him.

Now while these things were happening, his own lord had sent three messengers forth from the land to seek him; for he was harassed in war, endangered and hard bestead, so that he was losing all his castles, and all his land was being wasted. Often had he repented of banishing Eliduc, through foolish hearkening to evil counsel; and the traitors who had accused and slandered and wronged the knight, he had cast out of the land, and into exile sent for ever. And now in his sore distress he sent for his vassal, commanding and adjuring him by the bond of homage between them, to come to his lord's aid in this time of sore need.

At these tidings Eliduc was sorrowful for the maiden whom he loved passing well, and who loved him with all her heart. His hope and intent was that their love might continue to show itself in the giving of fair gifts and in speaking together, without foolish trifling or dalliance; but she thought to have him for her lord, if she might keep his love, for she knew not that he had wife.

'Alas!' he cried, 'that ever I came here; too long have I been in this land! Would I had never seen it! I have come to love the princess Guilliadun so dearly, and she loves me so well, that if we must part, one of us will die, or perhaps both! And yet I must go, for my lord has summoned me by letter, and I am bound to him by oath; and then again – my wife! Now it behoves me to take heed, for I must depart without fail, and if I were to wed my love, the Church would interfere. Everything goes ill with me! God – how hard is this parting! But whoever deem it wrong, I will always deal rightly with her, doing her will and following her counsel. The king, her father, has peace now, and looks for no further war; hence, for my lord's need I must ask leave before the end of my time for abiding in this land. I will go speak to the maid, and show her all my case; and when she has told me her will, I will do it as far as I may.'

He tarried no longer, but went at once to the king to ask leave, relating to him what had happened and reading the letter from his lord, who was so hard-pressed. And when the king heard that Eliduc might in no wise remain, he became sorrowful and troubled in thought, and offered largely of his possessions, one-third of his heritage and of his treasure; if only Eliduc would remain, he would give him cause to be grateful all his life.

'Pardieu' said Eliduc, 'since my lord is now so op-pressed, and has summoned me from afar, I must go hence for his occasions, nor in any wise remain. But if you have need of my service, I will return to you gladly with a strong force of knights.'

For this the king thanked him, and with all cour-tesy gave him leave to depart, setting at his disposal all the treasures of his mansion, gold and silver, dogs and horses, rich and beautiful silk. Of these took he measurably. Thereupon he added to the king, as was fitting, that he would like to say farewell to his daugh-ter, if it pleased him. The king answered, 'With all my heart,' and sent forward a page to open the chamber door.

Eliduc went with him, and when the lady saw the knight, she called him by name, and said he was six thousand times welcome. He asked her counsel in this matter, briefly showing the need for his journey; but ere he had told her all, or taken leave, or even asked it, she turned pale and swooned for grief. Seeing this, Eliduc began to lament, and kissed her often, weeping sorely, and held her in his arms until she had recovered from her swoon.

'Pardieu' he said, 'my sweet love, try to bear what I tell you. You are my life and my death, and in you is all my comfort! And though I must needs return to my land, and have already taken leave of your father, I counsel that there be troth-plight between us, and, whatsoever befall me, I will do your will!'

'Take me with you,' she cried, 'since you will not stay longer! Or if you will not, I must kill myself, for never more shall I have joy or content!'

Eliduc answered tenderly that indeed he loved her with true love: 'Sweet, I am bound to your father by oath, from now until the term which was set, and if I took you with me, I should belie my faith to him. I promise you faithfully and swear that if you will grant me leave and respite now, and set a day afterwards, and if you wish me to return, nothing in the world shall hinder me, if I be alive and well. My life is all in your hands!'

When she perceived his great love, she granted him a term, and set a day when he should come and take her with him. In bitter grief they exchanged gold rings, and with sweet kisses parted. Eliduc went down to the sea, and with a good wind was quickly across.

Upon his return his lord rejoiced greatly, and likewise his friends and his kinsmen and many other folk; and above all his good wife, who was so fair and wise and gentle. But he was always thinking upon the love that overmastered him; and showed no joy or pleasure at all – indeed, he might never be glad again until he saw his beloved.

He kept his secret well; and yet his wife grieved in heart, and often mourned by herself, for she knew not what this might be. Again and again she asked him if he had not heard from some one that she had been false to him or had sinned against him while he was out of the land. She would most gladly prove her innocence before his folk, whenever he pleased.

'Wife,' he said, 'I charge you with no sin or misdeed whatsoever. But in the land where I have been, I promised and swore to the king that I would return to him, for he has great need of me. If my lord had peace, I would not stay here eight days longer. I must endure great anxiety before I may return, yea, never until that time shall I take pleasure in anything that I see; for I would not break my pledge.'

With this the lady let be. He went to his lord and so much aided and supported him that by his counsel the king saved all the land.

But when the time appointed by the maiden drew near, he made ready for his departure; and having brought the enemy to terms, he arrayed himself for the journey, and likewise those he would take with him. These were only his two nephews whom he loved especially, the trusty chamberlain who had brought the message, and his squires; he had no desire for other comrades. These few he made promise and swear to keep silence on this undertaking.

He put out to sea at once, and was quickly across in the land where he was so eagerly expected.

Now, for prudence sake, Eliduc took lodging far from the harbour that he might not be seen or recognized, and arrayed his chamberlain to bear word to the princess, that he had kept her command, and was now arrived; and when the darkness of evening had fallen, she should come forth from the city with the chamberlain, and he himself would meet her.

The chamberlain changed his dress for disguise and went on foot all the way to the city where the king's daughter was. He devised a means to be admitted to her bower, and greeting the maiden, said that her lover was come. Upon hearing these tidings she was all startled and confused, wept tenderly for joy, and often kissed the messenger. He said further that at eventide she must go with him, for all the day he had been planning their flight. In the darkness of evening they set out from the city, the chamberlain and herself – no more than they two. She had great fear of being seen, for she was clad in a silken robe, delicately embroidered with gold, and had wrapped about her only a short mantle.

But her lover had come to meet her, and was awaiting them a bow-shot's length from the gate, by the hedge that enclosed a fair wooded park. When the chamberlain brought her up, he dismounted to kiss her; and they had exceeding great joy together. Soon, however, he placed her on a horse, mounted, took the reins, and rode away at full speed. When they arrived at Totnes harbour, they embarked at once, he and his own men only, and the lady Guilliadun.

At first they had a favouring breeze to waft them across, and calm weather; but even as they were nearing the shore, there came a storm at sea, and a wind arose before them, which drove them far from their haven, broke and split their mast and tore all their sail. Devoutly they called on God, on St. Nicholas and St. Clement, and Our Lady, the Virgin Mary, that she entreat her Son to save them from death, and bring them safe to land. One hour backwards, another forwards – thus they coasted along, for they were in the heart of the tempest. And presently one of the sailors cried aloud:

'What shall we do? Lord, you have here with you the one for whose sake we perish! We shall never come to land, for you have lawful wedded wife, and yet bear away this other, against God and the law, against right and honour! Let us cast her into the sea, and we may arrive at once!'

At these words Eliduc in his wrath all but hurt the fellow. 'Thou dastard! 'he cried, 'wretch! foul traitor!

[101]

be still! If I could leave my lady, you should pay dearly for this!'

He held the princess in his arms, soothing her as best he could both for her terror of the sea and for her woe in hearing that her lover had wife in his own land. But she fell forward in a swoon, and continued in that state, all pale and colourless, neither reviving nor breathing. He thought of a truth that she was dead, and fell into bitter grief. He arose and went to the sailor who had spoken, struck him with a gaff and stretched him prone, then hurled him overboard, head foremost into the sea, where the waves swept the body away. Thereupon the knight took the helm, and so steered the ship and held it firm, that he made the haven and came to land; and when they were arrived safely, he cast anchor and put down the gangway.

And still the maid lay with the look of death upon her, so that Eliduc in his heavy grief longed to lie dead by her side.

But he asked counsel of his comrades as to whither he should take her, for he would not part from her until she should be buried with great honour and fair service, as became a king's daughter, in holy ground. His men were all perplexed and had nothing to say, so the knight bethought him what he should do. He remembered that near his dwelling, itself so close to the sea that it could be reached by mid-day, in the great forest which stretched round about it for thirty leagues, a holy hermit had had a cell and chapel for forty years. Now since he knew this good man, he resolved to take the maid thither and bury her in his chapel; and to give enough land to found an abbey, and to place therein a convent of monks or nuns or canons, who should pray for her unceasingly, 'God grant her sweet mercy!'

So he had his horses brought, mounted with his men, and taking oath of them not to betray him, rode away on his palfrey with his lady in his arms. They journeyed straight on, until they came to the chapel in the wood, where they knocked and called, but found no one to answer, or to open to them, so that Eliduc must needs make one of his men climb over the wall to unbar and open the door. Within they found the new-made tomb of the holy man, who had died eight days before. At this the knight was sorely troubled and distressed; and when his men would have made the lady's grave, he put them back, saying:

'This must not be until I have taken counsel with the wise folk of the land, as to how I shall sanctify the place for abbey or for monastery. Let us lay her before the altar here, and commend her to God.'

He bade them forthwith bring robes and prepare a couch, on which he placed the maiden whom he thought dead. But when he came to the parting, he thought to die of grief. He kissed her eyes and her face, saying:

'Dear, please God, never more will I bear arms or live out my life in the world! Fair love – alas, that you ever saw me; sweet dear – alas, that you came with me! Pretty one, now had you been queen perhaps, were it not for the true love and loyal, with which you loved me. My heart aches sorely for you! On the day that I bury you I shall put on the cowl; and at your tomb day after day cry out anew my grief!'

At last he left the maiden, and made fast the door of the chapel; and then he sent a messenger to his dwelling to announce to his wife that he was on his way home, but was weary and travel-worn.

Upon hearing these tidings she rejoiced greatly, and, arraying herself to meet her lord, received him in all kindness; yet she got but little joy of him, for his looks were so forbidding that none dared accost him, and he spoke no loving word.

He was two days in the house; and after mass in the morning went forth alone on the road to the forest chapel, where the damsel lay. He found her neither revived nor seeming to breathe, yet he marvelled in seeing her still white and red, with no loss of her fair colour, save that she was a little pale. In his bitter anguish he wept and prayed for her soul; and having prayed, returned home.

One day, when he went forth from the church, his wife set a squire to watch him, promising to give horse and arms if he would follow his lord and see where he went. And as she bade him, he followed unperceived through the wood, saw Eliduc enter the chapel and heard his mourning. When the knight came out again, the squire returned to his lady, and told her of all the cries of grief and lamentation that her lord had made in the hermitage. All her heart was stirred, and she said:

'Let us go at once and search through the hermitage. My lord must go, I think, to the king's court. This hermit has been some time dead, and though I know well that my husband loved him, he never would do thus for his sake, nor feel such lasting grief.'

For the time she let be; but that same day, after noon, when Eliduc went to the king's court, she came with her squire to the hermitage. When she entered the chapel, and saw the bed with the maiden, who was like a fresh-blown rose, she put aside the robes and gazed upon the slender body, the long arms, and white hands with graceful fingers slim and shapely, and then she knew verily why her lord was in such grief. Calling the squire, she showed him the marvel.

'See,' she said, 'this woman, like a jewel in her fairness! She is my lord's friend, for whom he is all sorrowful. I' faith, I wonder not, since so lovely a woman is dead! As much for pity as for love, I shall never again have joy!'

She began to weep and make moan for the maiden. As she sat lamenting by the bedside, a weasel ran from under the altar, and because it passed over the corse, the squire struck it with his staff' and killed it. He threw it upon the floor, but it lay there only while one might run a league, before its mate sped thither and saw it. And when, after running about the dead weasel's head, and lifting it with its foot, the little creature could not get its mate to rise, it gave signs of grief, and sped out of the chapel among the herbs in the wood. Here it seized in its teeth a flower crimson of hue, and returned at once to place it in the mouth of its mate. Within the hour the weasel came to life. When the lady saw this, she cried to the squire,

'Stop it! Strike it, good lad! Let it not escape!'

He threw his staff so that the weasel dropped the flower; whereupon the lady rose and picking up the pretty blossom, placed it in the maiden's mouth. And presently, as she waited there, the damsel revived and breathed, saying as she opened her eyes, 'Dear God, I have slept long!'

The lady gave thanks to God, and asked the maid who she was, and she answered:

'Lady, I am of Logres, daughter to a king in that land. I loved dearly a good knight, Eliduc, and he brought me away with him; but he did wrong in beguiling me, for he has a wedded wife, and neither told me of her, nor ever made sign of such a thing. And when I heard speak of this wife, I swooned in my grief; and he, most unknightly, has abandoned me all desolate in a strange land. He has betrayed me, though I know not why. Foolish is she who puts her trust in man!'

'Fair maid,' answered the other, 'there is no living thing in all the world that can give him joy! One may say truly that since he believes you dead, he has fallen into strange despair; every day he has come to look upon you, though deeming to find you lifeless. I am his wife, and indeed my heart is heavy for him. Because he showed such great grief, I longed to know whither he went, came after him, and found you. I have great joy in finding you alive; and will take you back with me and restore you to your friend. As for myself, I will release him from his vows, and veil my head!'

Thus the lady comforted her and took her away, at the same time sending a squire to go for his lord. He journeyed until he came to him, and greeting him courteously, told him what had befallen. Thereupon Eliduc waited for no companion, but mounted at once, and rode home that selfsame night. When he found his lady alive he rendered thanks sweetly to his wife, and was more glad than he had ever been before. Again and again he kissed the maiden and she him most tenderly, and they had passing great joy together.

When his wife saw their happiness, she accosted her lord and asked his leave to depart and be a nun in God's service; further, she asked him to give her part of his land whereon she might build an abbey, and said that he should marry the one whom he loved so much, since it was neither well nor fitting to maintain two wives, nor would the law permit it.

Eliduc granted this, and parted from her in all kindness, saying that he would do all her will, and would give her of his land. Thus near the castle in a boskage hard by the chapel and the hermitage, she built her church and monastic dwellings, and added thereto land enough and rich possessions, so that she might be well content to live there. When it was all finished, she veiled her head, and took with her thirty nuns to establish the new order of her life.

Eliduc wedded his lady; and on that day held feast with great honour and splendid service. They lived together many a year in perfect love, giving alms largely and doing much good, until at length they turned them to God wholly.

Thereupon, with good counsel and care, Eliduc built a church also near the castle but on the other side, and bestowed upon it the greater part of his land, and all his gold and silver. He placed there men or good religion to establish the order of the house; and when all things were ready, after no long delay, he gave himself also to the service of God Omnipotent. He placed his beloved lady with his former wife, by whom she was received honourably as a sister, was admonished to serve God, and instructed in the rules of the order.

Together they prayed God to show sweet mercy to their friend; and he prayed for them, sending messengers to know how it was with them and how each did. Much they strove, each singly, to love God with good faith, and so made a fair ending, by the grace of the True and Holy God.

The chivalrous Britons of olden time made a lay of the adventure of these three, that it might not be forgotten.

NOTES

Notes

PROLOGUE

page 3 *Priscian tells us.* Author of a famous textbook on grammar, the *Institutiones Grammaticæ*. He lived at the end of the 5th century, and his book was widely studied during the Middle Ages. The passage to which Marie alludes occurs at the beginning, where Priscian discusses at length the question of imitating the Greeks, but does not make the statement which Marie attributes to him.

page 3 *Might employ the whole resources of their wit.* Dante, in his *De Vulgari Eloquentia*, lib. I, i, speaks in somewhat the same manner of the literary language, saying that few acquire the use of it, 'because we can be guided and instructed in it only by the expenditure of much time and by assiduous study.'

page 3 *Keep himself from sin… spare himself great sorrow.* The author of *Renard le Contrefait*, writing in the early part of the 13th century, expresses in some detail a similar thought. He speaks of the advantage of leisure for the production of good literary work, and tells how people who read old stories and translate Latin into Romance, are able to put sin and sorrow away from them.

GUIGEMAR

This lay belongs to the same class of fairy stories as *Grælent*, *Lanvall*, *Guingamor* and *Désiré*, while traces of the influence of this type of tale are to be seen in *Dolopathos* (the seventh story in the collection), in *La Naissance du Chevalier au Cygne* (Publ. of the Mod. Lang. Assoc. of America, IV), and in *Partonopeus de Blois*. Less distinctly it appears also in certain features of the English *Generides* (translated from a lost French original), in *Emaré* (also from a lost French poem), and in *Mélusine*. It is alluded to in *Erec et Enide*, l. 1954 ff., and in the continuation of the *Perceval*, ll. 21,779, 21,857–79.

It appears then that the story was widely known in the 12th century, the date of most of the above-mentioned works, and that its influence extended into the 13th, and even later. It seems worthwhile to consider briefly (1) the relation of *Guigemar* to the other members of the group, and (2) the probable source of this type of story.

Professor Zimmer has shown (*Ztsch. f. fr. Spr. u. Litt.*, XIII, p. 8 ff.) that Guingamor and Guigemar are variant forms of the same name. It does not of course follow that the stories are identical, as there are frequent instances of different and inconsistent tales attaching themselves to one hero.

Comparing the five lays for resemblances and differences, we find:

1. *Guigemar* alone has the definite theme that contempt of love leads to excessive suffering through love. In *Lanvall*, *Grælent* and *Désiré* the suffering is caused by disobedience to the fairy mistress, while in *Guingamor* also this idea appears, though subordinated to the narrative of the knight's adventures.

2. *Guigemar* and *Désiré* alone have the introduction dealing with the hero's early life and education.

3. In *Guigemar* and *Désiré* alone we have the strange deer (though details and circumstances vary). In *Guingamor* a boar is used instead. *Lanval* and *Grælent* agree in omitting the incident.

[114]

4. *Lanval*, *Grælent* and *Guingamor* agree in having the wooing by the queen, though in the last, it is soon lost sight of, and in the other two it leads to the trial of the knight and his rescue by the fairy. In *Désiré* also he finally goes to fairyland with his lady, though under different circumstances. In *Guigemar* alone he wins the lady in battle and takes her away with him, to his own home apparently.

5. In *Guigemar* alone we have journeys across the sea, though in *Guingamor*, *Lanval* and *Grælent* there is a 'perilous river' to be crossed.

6. In the love episode itself, *Grælent* and *Lanval* agree, and, on the whole, *Désiré* though with several additions. *Guingamor*, though with a different arrangement of episodes, is also fundamentally the same. *Guigemar* is entirely different. Here the attempt is made to convert the fairy mistress into a mortal, and as she is the wife of a jealous old man, the love-story becomes an intrigue similar to that in the first part of Yonec, plus the account of the adventures at Meriaduc's castle, where the lovers are finally united.

From even this brief comparison, it appears that *Lanval* and *Grælent* are undoubtedly the same story, while *Guingamor* and *Désiré* are simply other versions of it with independent alterations and additions. *Guingamor* and *Désiré* both show features approaching nearer to *Guigemar* than the other two. It would seem, then, that in its first part *Guigemar* goes back to the source of *Guingamor* and *Désiré*, while, in the second, it depends upon an entirely different story of marital jealousy. It is the imperfect blending of the two that accounts for the many inconsistencies and obscurities in the lay. To mention only a few: the lady is mortal, yet she alone can heal the knight's wound; she has fore-

[115]

knowledge of the discovery of the love intrigue, yet is pow-
erless to prevent it; she is imprisoned for more than two
years, and escapes finally in a most mysterious way; she has
no control over the fairy ship, yet it serves her as well as her
lover; she lives in 'the capital city of that realm,' but neither
city nor realm has a name; the jealous husband is simply
dropped from the story, as soon as the lovers have escaped
from his castle. Especially obscure is the part played by the
hind: she is apparently much distressed, about to die of the
wound inflicted by *Guigemar*, yet through her he attains
his happiness. She does not conduct him to the ship, and
yet, unless she is in some way connected with the ship, it is
difficult to see how she plays any further part in the story.

Partonopeus de Blois, written by a contemporary of Marie, contains the story in the following form; the knight is
separated from his companions during a hunt, and is led
by a boar to the ship which conveys him, without visible
propelling agencies, to the land where he finds his lady. It
is noteworthy that she is not a fay, but a mortal who has
studied magic, that she sends the ship, that he loses her
through breaking a taboo, and wins her again in a tournament. These facts, when taken in connection with the
inconsistencies in *Guigemar*, suggest that the original form
of this version may have been somewhat along these lines.

From the numerous verbal resemblances, especially in
rhyme-words, among the five lays, *Partonopeus* and *Dolopathos*, we may infer that the minstrels, in retelling the
story, combined a degree of verbal memory with fresh material introduced for the sake of variety, according to their
own fancy and stock of experience.

The basic story can be paralleled in general outline and in some details in Irish, and to some extent in Welsh. In Irish, we have the hero-tales of *Connla and the Fairy Maiden* (Jacobs, *Celtic Fairy Tales*, and Joyce, *Old Celtic Romances*), *Oisin in Tirnanoge* (Joyce) and the *Voyage of Bran*. Of these, the first and last are older than the lays, and the second, though modern in form, bears the marks of considerable antiquity. *Oisin* and *Bran* share with *Guingamor* the feature of a return to earth after an abode in fairyland. There is a group of similar stories in Welsh (Rhŷs, *Celtic Folklore*), and there are several told in much the same manner in Map's *De Nugis Curialium*, twelfth century, distinc. II, cap. xi–xiv, and IV, viii–xi), in which a fairy comes out of a lake, or in a boat, or appears by the lake-side, or in the forest, and wins the love of a shepherd or farmer. In most of these she is lost through the breaking of a taboo, though in others he is taken away to fairyland and never heard of again, and in one, at least, he returns after seven years.

Several episodes are paralleled repeatedly in Celtic literature. The magic deer (or sometimes boar) into which a fairy transforms herself, or which is under her control, is especially common. Finn's fairy sweetheart, in *The Colloquy* (O'Grady, *Silva Gadelica*, p. 163), could take the form of any animal she pleased. In *The Chase of Slieve Fuad* (Joyce) is a doe, 'very large and fierce, with a great pair of sharp, dangerous antlers,' which is used by an enchantress to decoy certain heroes. In Jensen's *Eddystone*, in *The Chase of Slieve Cullinn* (Joyce), and in various other Celtic tales, a hind of supernatural origin occurs; and in various other mediæval works, as *Tyolet* and Gottfried's *Tristan*, we find similar strange beasts. Another sort of parallel is furnished by Giraldus Cambrensis (cf *Introduction*, page xx) in his story of the Welsh hunter who received such sore bodily injury upon killing a hind with stag's horns. Again, we find still another sort of parallel in the Scots-Gælic *Leeching of Cayn's Leg* (Jacobs, *More Celtic Fairy Tales*), in which the heroine appears first as a roe-buck, and later, when her husband has broken three promises which she exacted of him, turns into a filly and wounds a man, by kicking him in the thigh, so that he can be healed only by a magic salve.

According to the oldest recorded Irish version of this same tale, given in *Silva Gadelica*, p. 332 ff. of the translation, O'Cronigan meets the fairy in the woods, and she takes refuge in the form of a hare in his bosom, promising him the dearest boon he could ask in return for his help. He deserts his own wife and lives with the fairy very happily for three years. Then at a feast which O'Cronigan gives, Cian falls in love with her, and when she refuses to be his, he knocks her down, whereupon she becomes a mare and rushes to the door. It is when he tries to stop her that she kicks him and injures his leg, so that no leech can heal it. At the end of a year his nephew brings him a salve which cures him, apparently a magic salve, though this is not perfectly clear. This older version is interesting because the logic is clearer between the transformation of the woman and the wounding of the man. And, again, the flight of the fairy when she is struck affords an interesting suggestion at least of the taboos (in Map and Rhŷs) laid upon the husband by the fairy-wife, not to strike her.

A similar story forms the opening of *Macphie's Black Dog* (*Scottish Celtic Review*, I). It is in his introduction to this that Campbell makes a statement which throws considerable light on the part played by the hind, which is, that the belief is common in the Highlands that deer are the fairies' cattle; hence arises the hostility of the fairies towards deer-hunters, and hence, also, their predilection for transforming themselves into deer.

The marvellous hind then is clearly a fairy, who being wounded to the death while in this form (and that fairies became mortal during their transformation is shown repeatedly – cf. *Yonec*, also *Macphie's Black Dog*, in which the fairy shows her true form as soon as the gun is pointed at her, and becomes a stag again as soon as it is lowered), takes her revenge on *Guigemar* by choosing, perhaps, what she considers the most unlikely mode of healing for him. It is difficult to see why the wound in the foot should be fatal; either this was the one vulnerable spot, or perhaps the arrow was poisoned.

In *Partonopeus* the boat was sent by the lady, and as the lady in this story was, according to *Erec et Enide*, l. 1954 ff., no less a person than Morgain la fee, the fairy queen herself, it is very probable that originally she sent the boat to save the knight.

A magic boat appears in *Connla*, in the *Fate of the Children of Turenn* (Joyce), and in one of the Welsh versions (Rhŷs I, p. 17).

The theme of the jealous husband is too common to be definitely localised. As it is treated in *Guigemar*, however, its resemblance to *Yonec* is noteworthy, the greatest differences being that the lover comes in a magic boat instead of as a bird, and when the intrigue is discovered, is turned adrift in the hope that he may perish, instead of being killed outright. Ahlström's arguments (*Stud. i. den. fornfr.*

Lais-Litt.) that this part of the lay shows Oriental influence have not been generally accepted.

Although the parallels given belong entirely to Great Britain, critics agree that the names used point to a Breton origin for the lay. Guigemar's home is in Léon, a province in the north-west of Brittany. His name had been borne by five lords of Léon, two of whom were famous men and contemporary with Marie; Hoilas is Hoel or Howel, the name of six dukes of Brittany, though Marie probably refers to the Arthurian Hoel, mentioned in Wace and Geoffrey of Monmouth; and Meriaduc was the name (Conan Meriaduc in full), of a mythical leader of the fifth century, under whose rule the (fabulous) conquest of Brittany was accomplished, as we read in Geoffrey of Monmouth.

Meriadoc is the name of one of the traitors in several versions of the Tristan story. He is also the hero of the French romance, *Li Chevaliers as Deus Espees*, and of the Latin prose *Vita Meriadoci* (edited by Professor Bruce). However, there seems to be no connection between any of these stories and the Meriaduc in *Guigemar*; indeed, they are all associated with Wales, while, according to Marie, Meriaduc lived in Brittany. That there was a well-known castle bearing his name, near St. Pol-de-Léon, seems certain. It is mentioned in the prologue to the *Vie de Saint Goëznou*, written 1019, as *Castrum Meriadoci* (De la Bordene, *Hist. de Bret.*, II, p. 526); and again, in a fourteenth-century Latin poem as *semirutum* (half-ruined) *castellum Meriadochi* (De la Borderie, III, p. 389). There may well have been traditions about Meriadoc current in Brittany, one of which served as a basis for this part of the story, or Marie may have laid the scene at this castle because it was a familiar landmark.

NOTES

Summing up, we may say, I think, that *Guigemar* is a composite of a story belonging to the *Lanval–Guingamor* group, but varying in the direction of *Partonopeus*, and of a story similar to the first part of *Yonec*. Moreover, it seems probable that the combination was not made before the middle of the twelfth century, that is, if not due to Marie herself, it must have been made by her immediate predecessor. Among the reasons for believing this are: (1) Conan Meriaduc is scarcely known in literature before Geoffrey of Monmouth; (2) the hind episode as related by Marie would be far more telling after the similar episode had been related in connection with Henry II; (3) the signs of welding are still so very apparent. If the two stories had been long handed down together, these signs would have disappeared before the story reached Marie, and hence became fixed in its final literary form. As it is, the lay seems to mark a transition from the old simple folk-tale in the direction of the elaborate episodic romance.[*]

page 7 *Who uses her time – to speak ill is their nature.* An attitude very similar to Marie's towards her work is shown by the poet Renart in his introduction to the *Lai de l'Ombre*. His general line of thought is: that he would rather employ his wit in good composition than be idle; and instead of tearing down the work of others, will build up some good thing, some pleasant work, even although churlish folk should scoff at him for employing his 'courtesy' in this way; for he is foolish who stops because of

[*]   For further reference and discussion on the sources of the Lays, see Köhler's *Vergleichende Anmerkungen*, with Warnke's additions, in Warnke's second edition. For this poem especially see Schofield's *Lay of Guingamor*, in *Harvard Studies and Notes*, V.

mockery or blame; if any wretch sticks out his tongue at this work, he is acting only according to his nature.

The comparison of a churlish backbiter to a dog occurs also in *Le Donnei des Amants*, ll. 67–75 (*Romania*, xxv): 'The mastiff and the churl in body and in nature are much alike. A dog shows friendliness by wagging his tail, then bites with his teeth – and a churl does much the same. When the churl most flatters you, beware lest he do you mischief; and when he shows you honour, 'tis not from courtesy, but from fear.'

page 7 *Noguent*. Curiously enough the sister is introduced and named, though Marie frequently has no names for her principal characters (out of fifty important characters only sixteen have names), and then dropped from the story. Perhaps originally Noguent's story also was given.

page 10 *Solomon's work*. The details of the ship bear some resemblance to *Partonopeus*, ll. 701–59. The phrase 'Solomon's work' is explained by several passages in the later *Grand S. Graal* (cf. Lonelich's version, E. E. T. S., chap, xxviii, pp. 353–65; chap, xxx, pp. 390–404; chap, xxxi, pp. 412–17), in which occurs a description of the ship built by Solomon, an account of its building and its symbolism. In the *Grand S. Graal*, Solomon builds the ship for the perfect knight who is to come of his line, and puts in it David's sword and crown with various other things for his use. When the symbolism of the ship is fully explained, we learn that it represents the Holy Church, and the sea, the world; the bed is the Holy Altar, also Christ's Cross, and so on. No one may enter the ship unless he is full of faith, and the moment he loses faith it splits; otherwise, it cannot be injured. It is not to be supposed that Marie intended to imply the elaborate symbolism found in the *Grand S. Graal*, nor is it certain that it even existed in her day; but she may have read some legend of a fine ship built by Solomon, and carried in her mind a few of the details. But the phrase more probably refers to the kind of ornamentation. (See Du Méril, *Floire et Blanceflor*, l. 556, where a marble tomb is inlaid with gold and silver *de la trifoire Salemon*; also, Förster, *De Venus la Deesse d'Amour*, st. 214, where an ivory saddle is inlaid *trestot de l'uevre Salemon*.) Perhaps I Kings, chap, vi, with its description of Solomon's Temple, which was so largely 'overlaid with gold' may have given rise to the term.

page 11 *Whoso placed his head upon it.* The pillow suggests one in *Generydes* (ed. Furnivall, ll. 291–326):

> Vnder whos heid it lay a stound,
> With what sekenes he wer bound,
> As long as it vndre him lay,
> Shuld noon yuell doo him betray.

page 12 *Ovid's book.* While the book of Ovid mentioned is evidently the *De Remedio Amoris*, it seems not impossible that the painting which represented 'the ways and nature of love,' might have been in illustration of the far more famous *Ars Amatoria*. That Venus should be displeased with the *De Remedio* is, of course, natural. Her method of dealing with it is distinctly mediæval. She burns it as heretical works were burned, and 'anathematizes' all who should read it, or follow its teachings. These paintings show marvellous lack of diplomacy on the part of the jealous husband; but perhaps the description is entirely without reference to the situation.

page 18 *Churls that call themselves knights.* 'Villeins courteous' is the literal translation, and the meaning is, men of knightly rank who do deeds worthy only of 'villeins,' i.e., peasants. The aristocratic tone is characteristic of Marie.

page 19 *Plait in it a fold – whoso could open the buckle thereof.* The plait and girdle, though probably originally magic, scarcely need to be so considered here. They do not occur in any other form of the story, and bear only a remote resemblance to other similar objects in mediæval or classical literature, as, the Gordian knot, and the knot taught Ulysses by Circe (*Od.* viii, l. 448); and the girdle in the *Bevers-saga*. It is noteworthy that in *Generydes* (ed. Furnivall), ll. 539–47, 605–20, 2325–2488, and *Generides* (ed. Wright), ll. 190–6, 1163–1253, Aufreus's shirt-sleeve is stained by the tears of his mistress, and can be washed clean only by herself; and it is by this means that, after a long separation, he finally discovers her.

page 20 *A great beam of pine.* The great beam which *Guigemar* seizes but does not use, may be a survival from a more primitive form of the story.

THE ASH TREE

This story falls into two distinct parts: the first hinges upon the common mediæval belief that it was impossible for a virtuous wife to have twins, and the second is the theme of the patient resignation of a man's love by a woman who has the best claim to it.

The lay as it stands is unique, but the elements of which it is composed were familiar matter in the Middle Ages. The first part appears in many forms in various popular tales, especially in Germany. In a large number of cases, the story is simply that a lady of rank reproves a beggar woman who has had twins or triplets, and is herself punished by having many more children at a birth. (For the titles of various collections of these popular tales, see Warnke, second edition of the *Lais*.) In a Dutch version (in the *Chronicle* of Hermann Korner published in Eccard's *Corpus historicum medii ævi*, II, pp. 955–956), one lady of rank accuses another and is the cause of her husband's putting her away. In this feature, it is manifestly nearer to *The Ash Tree* than the preceding forms of the story, though in its details widely different. In a Danish ballad (Grundtvig's *Danmarks garnie Folkeviser*, V, 386, No. 285 E), there is no question of slandering a neighbour, but the woman is punished for making, in public, a general statement similar to that in *The Ash Tree*; and, as in the lay, she tries to get rid of one child (here by throwing it into the water). There is also a Spanish romance in which it is the law that all mothers of twins should be burned or cast into the sea. The queen has two sons and disposes of one of them by putting him into a casket with gold and jewels, and letting this drift out to sea. Like *Le Fraisne*, he is named from the place where he is found, *Espinelo*, from a thorn-bush where the waves cast him ashore. Similar is the Italian poem *Gibello* in which the child, instead of being thrown into the sea, is given to foreign merchants whom the nurse happens to meet.

This story early became blended with the story of the man who married a swan-maiden, whose children were either monstrous, or were reported to be so by her mother-in-law, who thus took opportunity to wreak her malice. This is the case in *Le Chevalier au Cygne et Godefroidde Bouillon*, published by Baron de Reiffenberg, as may be seen by a comparison with *La Naissance du Chevalier au cygne*, where something of the wife's supernatural character is retained. Upon a prose version of the former romance depends the English prose *History of the noble Helyas, Knight of the Swanne*, and the Dutch folk-book of the *Ridder met de Zwan*.

In another French romance, *La Chanson du Chevalier au Cygne et de Godefroi de Bouillon*, published by Hippeau, the king laments that he has no children, upon seeing a woman with twins, whereupon the queen* makes the spiteful remark that occurs in *The Ash Tree*, and is punished by having seven children at once. This poem is the source of a Latin *Historia de milite de la Cygne*, published in de Reiffenberg's edition, and of the English Romance of the *Cheuelere Assigne*.

In still another group of stories this motif is combined with an attempt on the part of a jealous mother-in-law to separate her son from his wife by proving that the wife has really been false to her husband. Here belong the Italian *Libro di Fioravante*, the story of which occurs also in the *Reali di Francia* (Libro II, cap. 42), and the French and English versions of *Octavian*.

The second part of the story seems to have been widely known. It bears a certain general resemblance in idea to the story of Griselda, as told by Petrarch, Boccaccio and Chaucer, but varies so utterly in its details that it cannot be regarded as the source of these, in which the heroine is really of humble birth, is the wife of the hero, and is put aside

*   However, as the queen is found by the king on a hunting-trip, when he stops to rest by a fountain in a wood, much as in *La Naissance*, presumably she was originally a fairy in this case also.

temporarily, after she has endured patiently various other trials, only as a crowning test of her wifely obedience.

There is a ballad, found in Danish, Swedish, Dutch, German and Scotch, which bears a stronger resemblance to the second part of *The Ash Tree*. In this, the heroine is kidnapped when a child by robbers who sell her to the knight, though in the Scottish versions he himself stole her. After they have lived together many years and have had seven children, he puts her aside on account of her unknown birth, or because he can get more 'gold and gear' 'from another, and marries her sister; but the recognition comes in time. In several of the Scotch versions, the bride suggests driving her away, a trait which may have been suggested by the mother-in-law's attitude in Marie; and in one Swedish and one Dutch version, the brooch by which she was recognised was one which she had when she was stolen – a detail, perhaps, derived from the episode of the ring and the mantle (cf. Grundtvig, *Danmarks garnie Volkeviser*, V, p. 13 ff., and Child's *Ballads*, II, p. 63 m)

While there seems no reason for doubting that this lay is derived from a Celtic source, – indeed, the details concerning the lay sung in *Galerent de Bretagne* as Breton in character, increase the probability of this – it does not seem to have been as widely diffused as some of the other lays. That the episode of the twins is only an introduction, which did not belong originally to the story, is shown by the ballads; and when this is put aside, the tale is found elsewhere only in this group of ballads. M. de la Borderie suggests (III, p. 223) that it may be a local legend attaching itself to the village of La Coudre, about two leagues from Dol, which in the Middle Ages was a flourishing community.

page 32 *He who slanders another.* There are similar proverbs among Marie's *Fables*: 'Therefore no one ought to find fault with, or blame, the deed of another, nor bring another into ill repute; let each criticise himself! One may easily reprehend another's deed, who ought to be chiding himself' (No. liii); also, 'Such people secure the ill of another in such a way that the same comes upon themselves' (No. lxviii).

page 33 *Spangled silk.* Literally wheeled, i.e., covered with wheel-shaped ornaments, a design popular at that time.

page 36 *Le Fraisne.* Cf. *La Coldre*, page 38. In the names is indicated the popular origin of the tale. Names are given from some physical peculiarity or from some circumstance connected with the early history of the child. Cf Cinderella, Snow-White, Gold-Tree, Silver-Tree, Tom Thumb, Little One-Eye.

page 38 *Espouse a lady of noble birth.* He could not marry Le Fraisne because of her unknown origin. The Middle English translation (Weber's *Metrical Romances*, I, l. 312) explains this: 'Of was (whose) kin he knewe non.' The same reason is suggested in most of the ballads.

page 38 *They would not hold him as seigneur.* A similar instance of the power of vassals over their liege-lord is seen in the story of Pwyll, Prince of Dyved (Guest's *Mabinogion*), where the hero is counselled to put away his wife because she is supposed to have murdered her child.

page 39 *The Archbishop of Dol.* The allusion to the Archbishopric of Dol gives one limit for the date of the poem, as this See was suppressed in 1199.

page 40 *Bofu.* An unknown kind of rich cloth, usually mentioned in connection with silk, vair, gris. See Godefroy, *Dictionnaire de l'Ancienne Langue Française*.

page 41 *Laying aside her mantle.* This was a mark of re-spect at that time, probably symbolising a willingness to serve. Cf. page 40, where the act is simply one of conve-nience.

THE TWO LOVERS

This story seems to be a local legend (see Introduction, page xii) which exerted no appreciable influence upon mediæval literature. It is perfectly well known among the peasantry of the district to-day, as I ascertained by inquiry, and is said to be published under the title *L'Histoire des Deux Amants*, perhaps a modern chap-book. The story survives also in a series of paintings, dating apparently from the early part of the 19th century, which are preserved in the chateau built out of the ruins of the old 'Prieuré des Deux Amants.' This monastery stood until the 18th century on the summit of *La côte des Deux Amants*, the 'mountain marvellous high' (350 feet above the Seine and fairly steep, so much so that one part of the ascent is by a series of winding steps cut out of the turf).

No connection can be established between the present-day popular version and older folk-lore. It is possible that the modern form has a purely literary ancestry, and is de-rived from Marie. This much may be said: at the end of the 18th century, the story was revived by the poet David Du-val de Sanadon in a so-called 'fabliau,' *L'Origine du Prieuré des Deux Amants*, which is known to have had a purely literary origin and to depend ultimately upon Marie, but whether the modern popular version is derived from these literary productions or is a faint and far-away reflection of

Marie's source, it is impossible to say, without examining the popular version.

The lay contains several hints that Marie herself may have used a literary source. The most important of these is the use of the word *Neustria*. After the time of Charlemagne it was used only in an historical sense. Marie seems to have found it necessary to translate it for her hearers; it is therefore extremely improbable that it would have been used by the people. Moreover, it was used several times by Wace, in phrasing very similar to Marie's (*Roman de Rou*, ll. 94, 141–2, 1189). It occurs also in Geoffrey, but only once and without explanation. This is one of a number of slight links by which Marie's work seems to be connected with the works of these two men. It was, of course, almost inevitable that she should have read them.

While it may be that *Neustria* is only a touch of pedantry borrowed by Marie from Wace, there are several grounds for holding that she may have got the story from some narrative attached to the history of the priory. This was known by its curious name as early as 1031, when it was mentioned in connection with a grant of land. There are several theories to account for the name: one, that it was applied spiritually to a sculptured group of Christ and Mary Magdalen – it was dedicated to the latter – over the door; another that it was originally *des deux amonts*, from the fact that it stood in the angle formed by two intersecting ranges of hills. However this may be, in popular tradition (La Rochefoucauld, *Not. hist. sur l'arrond. des Andelis*, pp. 54–6) it was founded in the 12th century over the tomb of the lovers. This tradition may be based entirely upon Marie; but on the other hand, the stress which she herself puts upon the tomb, both at the beginning and at the end of her poem, rather suggests that this was a familiar object in her day, especially when it was taken in connection with the fact that the site of the chapel wherein stood the tomb of the lovers is still pointed out as being occupied by the library of the present chateau. It is not impossible that some such story as Marie's original may have been fabricated, or, if it already existed, attached to the priory to explain its origin. This would obviously attract attention to the priory, and would bring travellers there, to its profit. And again, this process was not unknown in the Middle Ages. The Abbey of St. Albans in England attached stories of the two Offas to its early history to enhance its greatness.

It is a curious coincidence that the hill is said still to furnish a few rare botanical specimens. The Marquis de Blosseville (*Extraits du Précis des Travaux de l'Académie impériale des Sciences, Belles lettres et Arts de Rouen*, année 1867–8, p. 525) states that M. Prévost found two, one of which was *Phytheuma orbicularis*, or herb of love. This rather points towards a confusion in idea of the potion from Salerno with the plants supposed in popular tales to spring from the graves of lovers who come to a tragic end. In Duval's poem it is said that popular superstition makes this 'an herb of love, a philtre of happiness'; but the authority for the statement is unknown.

The story, as Marie tells it, contains undoubtedly an allusion to the popular mediæval tale of the king who fell in love with his own daughter, the earliest known form of which is the late Greek romance *Apollonius of Tyre*. For English versions, see Gower, *Confessio Amantis*, book, viii, 1. 271 ff., ed. Macaulay, *Pericles, Prince of Tyre*, included

[131]

among Shakespeare's plays, and *Emaré*. For other versions, see Suchier, *La Manekine*, p. xxv ff.) I see no grounds for determining whether the allusion is a survival from an older form of the story, suppressed by Marie, or her source, or whether it has been introduced as a plausible reason for the king's decree. Perhaps the balance of probability lies with the latter, partly because there seems no adequate motive for suppressing so popular a story, and partly because its very familiarity in the minds of Marie's audience would seem to justify the allusion. Moreover, the Apollonius story, though undoubtedly of different origin, has the further resemblance that the king sets a riddle to all the wooers of his daughter, which they must guess in order to win her, and he fully believes that the solution is impossible. From this it is easy to see how the motive for the task of the one story could be transferred to the other.

The notion of a task set for the lover by the father of his beloved is not uncommon. It is found in several Greek tales (see Rohde, *Der Griechische Roman*, p. 420). A closer resemblance to the form of the task as given in the lay is found in a Persian story (Liebricht, *Zur Volkskunde*, p. 108 ff.), wherein the lover must run an incredibly long distance to win the lady, and drops dead before he reaches the goal. In an Egyptian story (Maspéro, *Contes de l'ancienne Egypte*, p. 33 ff., and Petrie, *Egyptian Tales*, second series, p. 13 ff.) the princess is in a house seventy cubits from the ground, and her hand is to be given to the suitor who succeeds in climbing up to her.

The only trace of direct influence by the lay, or its original, that has been noted, is a Calabrian love-song of the present day (quoted in a German translation by Warnke),

in which the hero is to win his sweetheart only on condition that he carry her in his arms, without resting, over
twelve high mountains.

page 49 *Salerno.* In Salerno, 34 miles south-east of Naples,
was the most famous medical school in Europe at this time,
the so-called *Civitas Hippocratica.* It was especially well
known to the Normans, being the centre of their power in
Italy until 1191, when the court was transferred to Palermo.
After this time Arab influence came gradually to domi-
nate, and by the middle of the 13th century, had usurped
completely the position held by the school of Salerno. Two
facts are interesting in connection with the allusion in the
lay: (1) that the school was especially celebrated for its
preparations of drugs, and (2) that the women physicians
were quite as famous as the men. An interesting illustration of this last fact is seen in Rutebœuf's poem *Le dit de
l'Erberie* (Méon, *Fabliaux et contes,* and Bartsch, *Chrestomathie*) which purports to be the speech of a travelling-physi-
cian, one of the followers of the celebrated Trotula (*Dame
Trote*) who flourished in the 11th century. References to
this school are common. Marie alludes to it again in her
Fables, and in Gottfried von Strassburg's *Tristan,* ll. 7333–5,
the wounded hero, wishing to conceal the fact that he is
going to Ireland to be healed, gives out that he is going to
Salerno.

YONEC

This lay is undoubtedly founded on a folk-tale, many versions of which are known throughout Europe. According to one form of the story, *L'Oiseau Bleu* told by the Countess d'Aulnoy in the 17th century, the princess is shut in a tower by her step-mother, and her betrothed visits her in the form of a blue bird, being compelled to take this form by the enchantment of a malevolent fairy. The step-mother upon discovering these visits, places within the tree on which he alights, which faces the lady's window, swords, knives, razors and daggers. He is severely wounded but not killed, and later, the princess is set free, finds him in human form in his own kingdom, and, convincing him of her innocence in his injuries, weds him.

In another and more modern version, told in Italy, Austria, Portugal, Austria, Greece and Denmark (for references, see Warnke), the prince assumes the bird-form at will and lays it aside in the presence of the lady; and again, he is not healed until the lady in the course of her search for him learns the only way by which this may be accomplished.

The two great differences between both popular versions and *Yonec* are: (1) the treachery in every case comes through a woman (in *Yonec*, to be sure, she is a spy and assistant), the heroine being unmarried; (2) all the popular versions end happily, the revenge in the second part of *Yonec* not being called for, since the hero does not die.

The earliest known version of the tale is a pre-eleventh century Irish account. It is found as a part of *The Destruction of Dá Derga's Hostel* (see Mr. Nutt's article in *Folk-Lore*, II, p. 87 ff, and Mr. Whitley Stokes's translation in the *Revue Celtique* for January 1901). The heroine, who is condemned to death by her own father, wins mercy from the thralls who are to carry out the order. They therefore shut her in a house with no door but only a window and a skylight. Here she is seen by the followers of a king, who, being childless and knowing a prophecy that a woman of unknown race should bear him a son, believes that this is the woman and resolves to seek her in marriage. But before this can happen, she is visited by a man, who comes flying as a bird, through the skylight, and lays aside his bird-skin. He prophecies that she shall have a son by him, and tells what he shall be called. She then marries the king, the son is born and carefully reared. From this point the story is different, for the king dies and the bird-man does not re-appear, though when the young man is grown and is following some birds, these suddenly take human form and remind him of the taboo laid upon him by his father, not to kill birds, because of his relationship with them.

The Celtic form of the story is evidently imperfect and compressed; but enough remains to give Marie's lay a much longer pedigree than it seemed, at first, to have.

The idea of the transformation of people into birds, by means of enchantment or fairy-like properties in themselves, is common in Celtic literature. It occurs in the story of the *Children of Lir* (Jacobs, *More Celtic Fairy Tales*), in *The Sea Maiden* (Jacobs, *Celtic Fairy Tales*), and in the *Sick-bed of Cuchullin* (Arbois de Jubainville, *L'Epopée Celtique en Irlande*); also, in the wide-spread *Swan-Children* and *Swan-Maiden* tales which certainly have Celtic affinities, even if they are not Celtic in origin.

The second part of the story, after the wounding of the falcon, is an account of a visit to his kingdom. As to the nature of this realm, considerable confusion seems to have existed in Marie's mind. The entrance is through a cave, and suggests at once the Celtic fairyland within the hills, as well as the Teutonic supernatural dwellers in them, yet the hero dies (perhaps like Undine, made mortal through love?) and is buried in a great abbey on the road from Cærüent to Cærleon. Again, there is confusion, when we read that the lady followed him through the window (20 feet from the ground, and lined with sharp iron prongs!), and after a long journey on foot through the cave into his own land returned, apparently the same day, with a magic ring to make her husband forget the whole occurrence (in *Cuchullins Sick-bed* a draught of magic liquor served the same purpose). Later on, she arrives, with her husband and son, after a day's journey on horseback, at the place where he is buried – a much greater distance, with no cave and apparently nothing supernatural about the situation. Further, the knight's body has not been moved, for he is said to have been king of 'this land'. Another curious thing is, that the abbey is described as the 'fairest castle of that age'; perhaps we are to suppose that it was the knight's own castle, wherein the monks were established to keep watch over his tomb until the son should come. Altogether, the most natural conclusion seems to be, that the fairy tale of the first part is blended with a human story of murder and vengeance, and the sign of the junction is in this very confusion. As was noted above, *Yonec* is the only version that has the vengeance story, for which I have not been able to find any parallel thus far.

Mr. Nutt suggests that the story of the Wooing of Etain (*Voyage of Bran*, II) shows certain resemblances in general outline to *Yonec*. This tells of a rivalry between a mortal and a fairy (who has the power of transforming himself into a bird) for the love of a woman, and of a consequent feud which results in the overthrow of the race of the mortal. *Yonec* may well be a reminiscence of this or a similar story.

Luzel, *Légendes Chrétiennes de la Basse-Bretagne*, III, has the story of a girl who is turned into a blue bird; but, apart from this fact, it shows little resemblance to *Yonec*.

The scene of the lay appears to be southern England and Wales, Cærüent being probably Winchester, the British *cær* being the Latin *castra* which became *chester*. The Old English form was Wintanceaster. There is still visible the site of the British city, on St. Katharine's Hill, about a mile from the present town, an extensive earth-work crowning the hill-top. At the base of the hill are two small rivers, or rather two branches of the Itchen, while the numerous rivulets and the marshy state of the meadows may indicate that once there was a considerable river with 'crossing by ferry', which Marie clearly implies was not the case in her own time. The river Duelas in Brittany has been taken as the site by the followers of Zimmer; but against this it may be said that Marie's spelling is uncertain (other MSS. read *Dualas, Ditalas*), and that, as far as we know, no city of Cærüent is, or has ever been, located upon that river.

page 55 *Iceland. Yslande* in the French. *Yrlande* was much more familiar to the people of the 12th century, and, moreover, gives more point to the comparison which would then mean, from Lincoln (Nicole in the Anglo-Norman spelling – cf. *Tristan*, ed. Michel I, p. 138, l. 2835) to Ireland – i.e., from east to west in the British Isles.

page 57 *Plunged into the river of hell.* Perhaps a reminiscence of the dipping of Achilles into Lethe, which made him invulnerable.

page 58 *I could not have come to you.* So Lanvall's fairy mistress comes to him only when he wishes for her.

page 58 *I will make myself like you.* The power of taking on the appearance of another person is illustrated also in the story of *Pwyll, Prince of Dyfed* (*Mabinogion*, pp. 339, 341–4), where the hero exchanges appearance and kingdom with a fairy king for a year.

page 63 *Cave.* Fairyland is often represented as across a river, or as an isle in the ocean. The classic parallels are Hades and the Hesperides. The mediæval confusion between fairyland and the world of departed spirits is well seen in the Middle English poem *Sir Orpheo* (from a lost French lay) in which Eurydice is represented as Queen of the Fairies.

page 64 *Parks.* French *defeis*, i.e., enclosed spaces not open to the public. According to Godefroy, the word is so used in Normandy today.

page 64 *As soon as I shall die.* Although the knight's kingdom is described as fairyland, he is here treated as a mortal and his powers of transformation must be looked upon as due to magic. Probably Marie cared very little about his exact nature; the story was all in all to her.

THE NIGHTINGALE

A proof of the popularity of the story on which this lay is based is its appearance in several collections of tales. In the *Renard Contrefait*, 13th century, the account is apparently founded on the lay itself, while in the Latin (and

French) and English *Gesta Romanorum* different versions are given.

In the Latin (and French) *Gesta*, the hero is married to an old woman, the lovers' meetings have nothing to do with the nightingale, except that the hero is brought to kill the husband by considering his own possible fate at the hands of one who so brutally killed the bird in which his wife took pleasure; and after the death of his wife the hero marries his sweetheart. In the fact that the husband gave his wife the bird's heart to eat, there is the suggestion of the popular story which is told in *Ignaurès*, in the *Châtelain de Coucy* and in various other forms, of the serving of a knight's heart in this way – a suggestion which tends to identify the hero with the bird.

In the English *Gesta*, the connection between the two is yet clearer: the lover sings as well as the nightingale, and the lady who is listening to the former makes the latter her excuse for standing at the window.

In *Le Donnei des Amants* (see page 122 above) the identification is complete. Here Tristan is the lover, and, having been long separated from Yseult he steals into the garden at night and there imitates in his singing the nightingale, the popinjay, the oriole and the birds of the wood. Yseult hears him, and knowing him by the song, steals away from Mark and out into the garden to meet her lover. Though other birds are mentioned, it is especially the song of the nightingale at the close of summer (*Romania* XXV, l. 465 ff.) that Tristan imitates.

M. Gaston Paris believes that the story in the *Donnei* is based on a Celtic original, and suggests also the probability of some relation between this story and the lay. What the connection is, is difficult to determine. Certainly the Latin *Gesta* is the most garbled, yet even it had one episode which implied the identification of the knight with the bird; and it is only by this connection that the husband's act in killing the bird is adequately motived. Moreover, the death of the husband and happy ending for the lovers in which all versions of the *Gesta* depart from the lay and the *Donnei*, is just such a change as would be expected in popular adaptations of old stories, while Marie's version is in harmony with the tragic ending of the *Tristan*; again, it, like the episode in the *Donnei*, stops abruptly, leaving one with a sense of dissatisfaction, which would be quite absent if one could regard the little poem as belonging to a perfectly familiar story.

Considering the main idea in each case (1) the lover's imitation of the nightingale's song (*Le Donnei*), and (2) the lady's use of the nightingale's song as an excuse for meeting her lover (Marie), I find it easier to believe that the two lays were originally analogous than identical, and I cannot see that the one theme is more likely than the other to have been the primitive form out of which the other developed. My belief that they were only analogous, is strengthened by the fact that Marie associated the Tristan story with South Wales and Cornwall, and places the scene of *The Nightingale* in Brittany.

Traces of the story upon which the lay is founded occur in references in Alexander Neckham, *De Naturis Rerum*, in the English *Owl and the Nightingale*, and in a 15th-century French lyric (quoted in Warnke).

The Marquis de la Villemarqué, in his *Barzaz-Breiz*, published a Breton ballad called *Ann Eostik*, which was at one time thought to represent Marie's original; but later investigations, to show that it is rather based upon the lay itself, have been generally accepted. I subjoin a literal translation of the rendering into modern French, to show the great difference in treatment between the popular version and the court-poetry as represented by the lay.

The young wife of St. Malo wept yesterday at her window: 'Alas! alas! I am undone! My poor nightingale is slain!'

'Tell me, my young wife, why you arise so often from your bed, so often from my side at midnight, bareheaded and bare-footed? Why do you rise thus?'

'If I arise thus at midnight from my bed, 'tis to see the great ships come and go.'

"Tis surely not for a ship that you go so often to the window; 'tis not for any ships, two or three; 'tis not to look at them more than at the moon and stars. Madame, tell me wherefore you arise night after night?'

'I get up to go look at my baby in his cradle.'

"Tis not to look at your son asleep. Tell me no stories. Why do you arise thus?'

'Dear little old man, be not vexed; I will tell you the truth. 'Tis a nightingale that I hear singing every night on a rose-bush in the garden. 'Tis a nightingale that I hear every night, singing so gaily, singing so sweetly, singing so sweetly, singing so musically, night after night, night after night, until the very sea is still.'

When the old man heard this, he thought, and said to himself in the depths of his heart: 'Whether this be true or false, the nightingale shall be caught!'

And when the dawn grew bright, he went to find the gardener.

'Good gardener, now listen; there is something that vexes me. There is a nightingale in the garden that does nothing but sing all night long, so sweetly that he keeps me awake. If you have caught it by this evening, I will give you a crown of gold.'

Hearing this, the gardener put a trap in the garden, caught the bird, and carried it to his master.

And the old man, when he held it, laughed with all his heart, and still laughing he strangled it and threw it on his wife's knees.

'Hey now, my young wife, here is your pretty nightingale. For your sake have I trapped it; I hope, my dear, you are pleased.'

On hearing this news the young lover said very sadly:

'Lo, now, we are caught, my sweet and I! Never again may we look at each other in the moonlight at the window, as we were wont to do!'

(Translated from Hertz, *Spielmannsbuch*. Villemarqué's rendering varies in a few unimportant details.)

It is perhaps worth while to call attention to the fact that the modern ballad is not based entirely upon the lay. Marie represents the two knights as equals in rank and age. The *Gesta* versions represent the husband as old, the lover as young and poor. The Breton ballad lays much stress upon the difference in age between the husband, and his wife and her young lover. Certainly here is one trait peculiar to the popular versions found in a poem which in almost every other respect agrees with the literary version. It may be that it was arbitrarily transferred from the one to the other, or that the two became confused during the formation of the ballad; but it may also be that, notwithstanding its modern form, there is more that is ancient in the Breton ballad, than has generally been accredited to it.

THE HONEYSUCKLE

This lay is so distinctly episodic that it could have little interest for an audience unfamiliar with the story of Tristan and Yseult. Its dependence upon Celtic sources has been questioned chiefly on the ground of its episodic character; and Dr. Brugger claims that it is based upon the lyric *Lai du chievrefoil* (most accessible in Bartsch, *Chrestomathie de l'ancien français*, 3rd ed., p. 257), which in the Berne MS. is attributed to Tristan himself. An examination of the lyric, however, shows not the slightest reason for connecting it with Tristan. The scribe may easily have been led astray by the identity of title, knowing from Marie that Tristan had composed a lay on this subject. And the author states that he calls his poem *Honeysuckle* because it may be compared to the flower in its sweetness.

As to a Celtic source, it must be observed that Marie does not specifically state that she had this story from 'li Bretun.' She says only that she had heard many tell it, and had also found it in writing; further, that it was composed by Tristram, whom she associates with South Wales. Without concluding that the source was therefore Welsh, or, from the use of the English title *Gotelef* that it was English, we may note at least two facts which should be considered in dealing with the question: (1) undoubtedly lays of non-Celtic source were included among 'lays of Britain'; (2) so far as Marie's sources can be tested, there seems no reason for charging her with untruth at any point. She states that six of the lays were made by 'li Bretun' (*Guigemar, Equitan, Lanvall, The Two Lovers, The Nightingale*, and *Eliduc*), and implies this in the case of a seventh (*The Werewolf*). Of the other five, *The Unfortunate*, though the scene is laid in

[143]

Nantes, belongs essentially to the time of chivalry and has no deep roots in earlier lore – it may well have been based upon a real incident. *The Ash Tree* has the look of a local legend attached to the neighbourhood of Dol, but there is no certain proof; the other three, as far as we may judge from their content and relationships, attach themselves chiefly to Wales.

More especially with reference to *The Honeysuckle*, it may be noted that the sort of meeting there described, is similar to the meetings described by Gottfried von Strassburg, ll. 14,427–48. Upon the advice of Brangæne, Tristan cuts his initial and Yseult's into a piece of wood and throws it into the brook, which carries it through the garden to Yseult; and so he meets her in the garden. There is some likeness also to the two meetings of the lovers in the forest, as told by Eilhart d'Oberg, ll. 6527 ff. and 7620 ff.

Note also that Marie's statement, 'other times had she met him in this way,' might well allude to the scenes described in Gottfried and Eilhart. Altogether, it seems likely that these fragmentary lays may be based on Celtic sources; and the likelihood is perhaps rather increased by the fact that they do not exactly fit into the story as told by Thomas or Béroul. It is easier to suppose that they represent varying accounts (especially as both Marie and Thomas emphasise the diversity of narratives on the subject), than to suppose that they are, at this early period, inventions similar to the short lyrics interspersed through the later prose romance.

The exact subject of Tristram's lay, to which Marie alludes, is sometimes misunderstood, but her words are explicit: it consisted of what the queen said to him when they met, and it was for remembrance of her words that he made it. It is not impossible that the message on the hazel, of which the sentence beginning 'Sweet love,' p. 97, is quoted directly, may be the substance of another lay, and, indeed, as this is the only part of the poem that justifies the use of the title *Honeysuckle*, we must suppose either that this was the case and that Marie confused it or purposely blended it with the lay of Yseult's words, or that the two episodes were combined in the original lay.

page 77 *Many have told it.* There are numerous versions of the story in mediæval French, German, Norse, Italian, and English (Scots). The French versions (together with one in Greek) were published by M. Michel; the most important German versions are the poems of Gottfried von Strassburg (based upon the French poem of Thomas), of Eilhart d'Oberg (based upon the French version of Béroul). In modern times the story has been treated by Wagner, Tennyson, Arnold, and Swinburne.

page 78 *Hazel.* Divining-rods have most commonly been made of hazel, because of its supposed power of finding hidden things. Perhaps this may be the reason why Tristram chose it – to carry out the symbolism of the whole procedure.

page 78 *This was the import of the writing.* We cannot suppose that Tristram wrote out in full the message of which the 'import' fills seventeen lines. Even if it had been possible, Yseult could not have read it as she rode along, nor was there any need for her to do so, as the branch served merely to indicate Tristram's whereabouts. The message was probably conveyed to her by the symbolism of the hazel and the honeysuckle. The meaning of the passage seems to be that he cut out a four-sided piece (*quarree*, Latin *quadrata*), i.e., made a sort of tablet by stripping off (*pare*) the bark, and wrote his name within the space so marked. Cf. the Old English poem, *The Lover's Message*, with the combined initials at the end. In this case, however, the tablet was apparently cut out of the tree and sent to the lady. The Irish *Scél Baili Bimberlaig* (*Rev. Celt.*, XIII) shows several interesting points of contact with this lay. It tells of tablets, made out of wood that grew upon the graves of two lovers, upon which were written, in ogham, poems, chiefly of love. These tablets when brought together had such attractive force for each other that they twined together 'as the woodbine (honeysuckle) round a branch, nor was it possible to sever them.'

ELIDUC

This lay bears the stamp of considerable antiquity, both in the old popular superstitions contained in it, and in the original theme, which in admitting the practice of bigamy goes back to a primitive state of civilisation.

The story of a man who becomes involved with two women exists in at least four versions, in addition to *Eliduc*: in the German *Graf von Gleichen* which attaches itself to a 13th century tomb at Erfurt (first appears in 1539); in the French *Gilles de Trasignies* (romance of the 15th century, probably based on a poem of 14th); in the modern Gælic *Gold-Tree and Silver-Tree*, and in the romance of *Ille et Galeron*, finished about 1167, and founded on an earlier lay.

Graf von Gleichen, imprisoned by a Saracen king during a crusade, is restored to liberty by the king's daughter on condition that he marry her. He has already a wife, but nevertheless flees with the princess to Rome, where he obtains a dispensation from the Pope to keep both wives, and the two women love each other dearly.

In *Gilles de Trasignies* the story approaches closer to *Eleduc*, in that the hero wins his second wife by freeing her father from a war waged by an unsuccessful suitor for herself. Further, he marries the second wife in the belief that the first is dead, and when the real situation becomes clear, the first insists upon taking the veil. Thereupon the second wife does likewise, and the husband follows the example. The ending is very similar to that in *Eliduc*.

The modern Gælic story has an introduction in which a mother who is jealous of her daughter's beauty tries to kill her. She is, however, rescued and married to a prince in another land. But her mother learns of her whereabouts by means of a magic trout that she has, and following her up, succeeds in poisoning her so that she falls in a trance as if dead. She continues so beautiful that the prince keeps her in a room of his house, where she is discovered by a second wife whom the prince marries later on; and is restored to life by the removal from her finger of the poisoned stab that caused her death. The second wife then offers to depart, but the prince insists upon keeping them both. Afterwards the wicked mother is duly punished, and the three live together happily.

It appears at once that the trance incident is very much like Grimm's story of *Little Snow-White*.

In *Ille et Galeron* the hero leaves his first wife because he has lost an eye in a tournament, and fears that she will not continue to love him. He marries the second out of pity for her great love, in the belief that the first is dead; and when the latter finds him with his second wife, she takes the veil.

Comparing these five versions, we get the following results:

1. The introductory episode of the jealous mother is found only in *Gold-Tr.* (and is very evidently the *Little Snow- White* story); but it is connected with the trance, and in *Elid.* we have the trance, though its cause and its cure are different.

2. In *Gold-Tr.* and *Gleich.* only, we have the frank admission of bigamy, though in the former the first wife offers to give up her place; in *Elid.*, *Ille* and *Tras.* the first wife retires into a nunnery in favour of the second.

Certainly *Gold-Tr.* must represent the most primitive form of the legend, with *Gleich.* on the one side as a not altogether successful attempt to bring it within the Christian code, and *Elid.*, *Ille* and *Tras.* on the other, as somewhat closely related to one another, and as a far more successful solution of the problem.

As to the more detailed relationships existing among the five stories, the fact that the jealous mother, trance and bigamy elements are combined in *Gold-Tr.*, and the two latter (however modified) distinctly suggested in *Elid.*, while *Little Snow-White* seems to connect the two former closely, seems to indicate that all three entered into the original story. If this be true, in Germany it appears broken into two stories, *Snow-White* and *Gleich.*, while in France, only the bigamy part has been preserved (with the exception of the trance in *Elid.*).

Ille is based either upon *Elid.* or upon a lay, very similar to *Elid.*, having the same name as itself. In favour of the latter view may be urged l. 928 ff., which may be interpreted to agree with the latter theory, and also the fact that *Elid.* has both the storm at sea and the trance not found in *Ille,* while *Ille* has the loss of the eye not in *Elid.*

Both *Gleich* and *Tras.* seem to represent the arbitrary use of a legend to explain an historic fact – namely, the representation on a tomb of a man with two wives.

Of the various elements in the story as a whole, the bigamy certainly indicated a state of affairs quite common among the early Celts (see Mr. Nutt's article in *Folk-Lore* III, p. 26 ff.). A parallel to the situation is found also in the story of Amleth as given in *Saxo Grammaticus.* The circumstances are different, but the kindly reception of the second wife by the first is in agreement with the *Eliduc-*story. Moreover, in *Cuchullin's Sick-bed*, we find both the trance and the double marriage, though the two wives are far from harmonious – from which we may conclude not that this tale is a close parallel, but that the elements of which both stories are composed were familiar to the Celts.

The trance and restoration in *Gold- Tr.* and in *Elid.* show a fundamental difference. *Gold- Tr.* is very similar to *Snow-White;* in both it is a question of poisoning and of cure by the removal of the poisonous object. In *Elid.* the princess falls into a death-like swoon through a painful shock and is restored by means of a magic herb brought by a weasel to restore its dead mate to life. It would seem as if the original situation had become obscured and replaced by an incident very common in Greek literature (see Rohde, p. 125) in which it is very often a serpent that revives its mate. In Grimm's story *Die drei Schlangenblätter* this form of the story occurs. As to the kind of flower used, the bare suggestion may be given that according to Gayot, *Les Petits Quadrupèdes*, II, p. 194, the weasel preserves itself from snake-bite by means of vervain. As this flower was well known in popular flower-lore, and folk-medicine, and its color ranges through shades of purplish red, it is not impossible that it may be meant. The fact that the weasel protects itself by means of certain herbs against snake-bites is said to have been observed by Aristotle (Gayot, II, 194); hence, in mediæval lore, it may easily have been extended to mean against any form of death. Giraldus Cambrensis in his *Topog. Hibern.*, distinc. I, cap. xxvii, tells of weasels restoring their dead by means of a yellow flower. Cf. Hertz, *Spielmannsbuch*, note on this passage.

There is a curious incident in *Elid.* not found in any other version, and probably therefore extraneous, the proposition to throw the princess overboard, in order to enable the ship to advance. The notion of making a sacrifice to the sea, or of appeasing it by the death of a guilty person, is exceedingly old and very wide-spread. We find it in the story of Jonah, in the romance of *Tristan le Léonois*, in many ballads such as *Bonnie Annie, Brown Robin's Confession*, and the Norse, Swedish and Danish *Herr Peter*, in popular tales of France and Germany, in the *Pali-Jatakas*, a Buddhistic tale (see *Journal Asiatique*, série vii, xi, p. 360 ff.), in Greek and Latin stories (see Warnke, for references). In nearly every case, the guilty person, or the one to be sacrificed, is determined by lot; but in *Elid.* the princess, who is perhaps looked upon as the cause of Eliduc's sin, is pointed out directly for sacrifice. It is noteworthy that the ship does not advance towards the haven until someone is thrown overboard, the some one being the unfortunate sailor who suggested the need of this severe remedy. Moreover, it is curious to observe that he voiced the moral sentiments of the story, according to which Eliduc is plainly in the wrong, and yet he becomes the villain and is so treated, merely because he stands in the hero's way.

page 83 *But at last... in her land.* These lines contain a brief introduction in the form of a summary of the story, but with no indication of the outcome. This is true also of *Yonec*, and in *The Two Lovers* the tragic outcome is told. In *The Honeysuckle*, the theme of the whole story, of which the lay is not even an integral part, is given.

page 83 *It hight Eliduc at first.* The same uncertainty as to the naming of the lay is seen in *Le Chaitival, The Unfortunate*, which at first was to be called *Les Quatre Doels, The Four Woes*. In the latter case, Marie says, some called it by the one title and some by the other; but with *Eliduc*, she seemed to approve of the title *Guildeluëc and Guilliadun*, while admitting that the first title was *Eliduc*. One of the manuscripts reads *Guildeluëc ha Gualadun, ha* being the Cornish, Breton and Welsh equivalents of the old French *e, and*. The corresponding Irish forms are *acus* and *agus*.

page 84 *As the peasant says.* I have not found this curious proverb, among the numerous popular sayings attributed to the villein or peasant at this time. The sentiment is perhaps appropriate for a villein, but the language is curiously feudal.

page 84 *In his domain.* The source of *Eliduc* is claimed for Brittany, partly because of the name (an Elisuc was abbot of Landevenec in 1057, and Professor Zimmer states that the names are identical, and partly because the hero's home is in Brittany. It may be observed, however, that Geoffrey of Monmouth and Wace have an 'Aliduc,' whom they place at Tintagel, and the former has also a 'Mapeledauc,' i.e., son of Eledauc; and further, that the localisation on the Devonshire side is far more definite than on the Breton, where we do not know the name of Eliduc's residence, nor yet of his king's.

page 86 *Narrow pass.* There is a gap here of about two lines in the MS.

page 99 *Prove her innocence.* Perhaps by the ordeal of red-hot iron, as Yseult did (cf. Scottish *Sir Tristrem*, ll. 2278–86).

page 101 *St. Nicholas.* Of Myra. While on a pilgrimage to Jerusalem, he miraculously stilled a storm at sea, hence came to be the patron saint of travellers and merchants. On the Norman font in Winchester Cathedral this event is represented, together with three or four other miracles of the saint.

page 101 *St. Clement.* Perhaps Clement of Alexandria, who in Marie's day was still a saint, but has since been removed from the calendar. There was also a St. Clement, the first Bishop of Metz, whose life was written at least twice during the 12th century.

TIGER OF THE STRIPE

Typeset in the United Kingdom
by Tiger of the Stripe
in Adobe Jenson Pro,
Lucida Blackletter
and Eileen Caps

www.ingramcontent.com/pod-product-compliance
Lightning Source LLC
Chambersburg PA
CBHW021010180626
46814CB00003B/1229